NEW HAVEN

HIGHMIND SERIES

ROXANNE WARD

GO GO SELF PUBLISHING VW

Copyright

First Publication

Go Go Publishing

First edition

Idaho, USA, 2024

Published Date

Copyright © 2024 by Roxanne Ward

Cover design by RG GraphX Design and Russell Ward

ISBN paperback 979-8-9880010-3-4   ASIN Kindle eBook BODDFTRMQL

ISBN paperback 979-8-3304-8739-4   eBook with Ingram Spark ISBN 979-8-3304-8733-2

Genres: science fiction, speculative fiction, post-apocalyptic fiction, baseball fiction, mystery fiction, young adult fiction

Notice: This book contains no adult situations or language and is appropriate for all readers.

file 6

OTHER BOOKS

BY ROXANNE WARD

<u>Highmind series</u>

Somewhere Else Book 1

New Haven Book 2

Journey to Cali Bantu Book 3

<u>From Darkness series</u>

Sins of Survival Book 1

Lion's Creed Book 2

Recalamtion Book 3

To Carolyn and Delia

All great things are simple, and many can be expressed in a single word: freedom, justice, honor, duty, mercy, hope.

Winston Churchill

PROLOGUE

Haru Abar sat at the large conference table in New Haven's Town Hall building. As the town's Spiritual Leader and Head of the Mental Health Department, it was his job to settle the citizens in the newly established sanctuary. But the conundrum before him was anything but settling.

He contemplated the intricately made castle in the center of the table and the young boy in danger because of it. It was painted with stunning detail demonstrating its artist's skill, but its artistry was a façade. It held critical secrets the rebellion desperately needed. Secrets this child was fated to unravel.

His ethereal connection to the castle was severed when he heard the shuffling of footsteps in the hall. The doorknob turned and in walked Bannon Vogel and Gray Takota. Bannon was the creator and financial backer of the sanctuary town, and Gray was the commander of the Defender army.

"So, what's up, Haru, and why the urgent meeting?" Bannon asked as he sat down at the head of the table. Bannon was relieved that everyone and everything was secured in the tunnel, even though it would take months to be fully up and running. Gray had addressed the threat at the Hold, and there had been no sign they were discovered or there was any compromising knowledge of the site.

The doors were locked down, and the false nuclear accident had been accepted as truth. The nuclear generators they were using performed perfectly, and by emitting a faint amount of radiation it made the story all the more credible. All the known issues had been addressed, but as with any complex and secretive venture, the unknown loomed like a smoking volcano.

"We need to discuss Alec T," Haru said. The acronym was designed to look like a name that stood for the Alliance for Liberty, Ethics, Community, and Tenability. It was the group that spearheaded and constructed the New Haven project.

Bannon's cheerful expression turned on a dime, and Gray froze. Bannon looked down noticing the castle. He was formulating many questions about it, but its prominent placement indicated the meeting was about such answers, so he would wait. "Yes, go ahead."

Gray was still standing in the same position since the mention of the name. He didn't even sit down until Bannon had motioned him to. Keeping New Haven secure was his responsibility, and he was still concluding his reports on the incident at the Hold.

"I have been keeping an eye on the boy, Connor." Haru began. "I just wanted to be sure he wasn't exposed to ongoing sensitive information. He was aware of the boxes of art and architectural plans as well as the weapons and medicines his grandfather hid at his house."

"Many residents hid such supplies when warehouse raids made it impossible to keep large inventories of critical materials. Those things are common knowledge to the residents, and they are allowed to discuss their experiences." Gray said.

"I'm worried about one of the planning papers Connor found with the Alec T. stamp. That stamp didn't leave the tunnel, and very few people had access to stamped papers. It was only used at the highest level to confirm the final approval of plans. It was also a security measure to prevent sabotage. I think Connor saw it."

"How did he get it?" Gray asked.

"Good question," said Bannon. "as you know, his grandfather, Deegan, was a member of Alec T. and involved in the final approval steps. We were in disarray when he died in a sudden accident. Deegan had the papers in his secret wall shelf. We track those final papers on a chain of custody list. I don't know why we didn't notice it missing. I guess that paper fell through the cracks."

"Why do we think Connor noticed it, or that he remembers it? I mean, he's just a kid." Gray was leaning on his elbows with his hands folded in front of him.

"I wasn't worried until I saw his IQ scores," responded Haru. "We knew Deegan and his wife participated in the Highmind experiment when we screened him. The experiment to increase intelligence quotients failed on the initial participants, but a significant percentage of their offspring displayed extraordinary aptitude, continuing onto subsequent generations. Their daughter displayed average intellect, but Deegan's grandson displays incredible Highmind traits. I imagine Deegan recognized this when he was an infant and kept it hidden.

"Connor scores exceptionally high in spatial awareness and hyperthymesia," Haru saw everyone's questioning looks. "Hyperthymesia means his recall ability is off the charts. Other assessments suggest he is also quite artistic. He has not had much exposure to art beyond Deegan's sketchbook and the museum exhibit book he found." Haru opened the folder containing Connor's drawing of Vadina. "This is what he taught himself in just over a month and limited study time."

"These are extraordinary," Bannon said as he passed the drawings around.

"In my visits with him, I saw he possessed an exceptionally mature and methodical approach to problem-solving." Haru picked up the castle gently. "This would be a difficult puzzle for most adults, but he has made good progress without anyone seeing him. He accomplished two steps at his Fairplay home and one more while in the Hold. I designed the Hold to maximize social time, so he couldn't have had much time to be alone.

"I bet he needed the flashlight he borrowed from me for that step," Gray speculated as Haru put the castle near him to inspect it. He was recalling the seemingly average, wavy-haired kid who loved baseball. How could he have missed all this about him?

Haru went on. "His grandfather taught him to hide his mental abilities. He also taught the exact lessons required to solve the complex intelligence clues A.L.E.C.T. uses. I believe," Haru said while pointing, "this castle contains a clue to the whereabouts of Cali Bantu. "

Again, shocked faces filled the room while intense stares bore through the castle. The secrets of Cali Bantu were lost when every one of the original members of Alec T. died. It was assumed they fell victim to nefarious acts, not because the group had been discovered, but because of their age. Dailys didn't live past their fifties, and some died sooner if they displayed health or age-related issues. When Dailys reached the age of inefficiency, they fell victim to disease, disappearances, and freak accidents.

Haru continued. "Deegan was a top-notch architect and one of the founders of the underground group. Without his knowledge, we have little hope of finding Cali Bantu. We don't even know what it is, but many believe it is a powerful weapon. Whatever it is, we need to find it first."

The room sat in silence until Bannon broke the spell. "You could be right. My dad's diary never mentioned the location of Cali Bantu, but he knew some of the people who held pieces of that knowledge. He didn't disclose any names, but no one person knew it all. He used to say, 'The information will come from the pure of heart when the world is ready.' I used to laugh it off, thinking it was one of his political platitudes. Maybe it was a literal forecast of the plan to pass it on to the next generation. So, you believe Connor knows something about Alec T. and perhaps holds the key to the location of Cali Bantu?"

Haru nodded his tilted head with a regretful look on his face. "It's a lot for a young child to bear, and I'm sure it troubled Deegan to burden him with it. It must have been his only choice, but he taught his young grandson how to conduct a thorough search for answers and evidence which is how he discovered the shelf. He taught him the story of Camelot, so he could unravel this puzzle before us.

"Connor has a curious mind and a keen awareness of his surroundings. He is compelled to solve mysteries despite the dangers. When they removed the weapons and medicines from the concealed basement, he watched it happening through a mouse hole. With his sharp mind and enhanced memory, there is little doubt he missed a name on a document he was curious about. And even if he didn't pay attention to it then, he can recall every detail of the document later."

Bannon leaned back in his chair and tipped his head into his folded hands. He took a big breath, letting it out in a long puff of air. For several moments, he sat with a concentrated look on his face. The wheels in his head were visibly churning over the issue and weighing the possibilities. "Why would he not share that with you or ask about it?"

"He's quite good at keeping secrets. Unless it was necessary, he wouldn't divulge anything. His whole life has been one secret after another. He has hidden his Highmind status from his own parents." Haru had more to say, but Gray piped in.

"What exactly did the note say?" Gray was excellent at predicting human behavior and had a sharp mind for detail.

"Simply, 'Approved for construction. Alec T.' I figured he wouldn't care or try to remember, but today he was looking through the T section of the resident address list on his tablet. It may be just an innocent desire to connect with someone who knew his grandfather. There's no way he knows what A.L.E.C.T. means or how dangerous knowing about it is." Haru leaned on his folded hands, observing the men before him.

The three of them were the top rung of the government at New Haven. They were self-appointed officials due to the deception that brought them here. As honorable as these men were, Haru worried they would resist relinquishing the town to elected officials when the time came. But if they failed to do so, it could morph into an oppressive we-know-best governing system. The whole point of A.L.E.C.T. was to restore democracy. They couldn't let each other forget that.

"So, what we need to do is finish solving the castle and interpret what it reveals. And we need to come up with a convincing lie about Alec T. or solicit Connor's confidence," Bannon said, summing up the dilemma.

"Well, as far as the castle goes," Haru reported. "Rand looked it over and took an X-ray of it. If we try to pull it apart, it has a vial that probably will destroy whatever it is meant to disclose. If it does provide clues to Cali Bantu, we can't risk losing it."

Bannon rubbed his temples. "Well, I guess we should send for Connor." He picked up his tablet and pushed the buttons for the Wayther household. He had his earbuds in, so the other two men sat listening to half the conversation.

"Hi Henry, it's Bannon. I hope I didn't wake you. Oh good. Hey, I know it's the weekend, but I need to see Connor regarding an item we transported for him. Yes, it is nice to have weekends with family. No need to thank me. It was our pleasure. But I need to see Connor at the Town Hall building. It won't take long. Is he there? Great, thanks. I'll send a cart. You're very welcome. Bye." Bannon ended the call and rang his weekend secretary to send a cart to address 90. "He'll be here in ten. He had just returned from breakfast."

"As far as the Alec T. issue is concerned," Gray took over, "we can't tell him it's a country-wide organization to restore democracy or anything about Cali Bantu. As I see it, we have three choices. We can say 'he' died, didn't show up to the Hold, or 'he' isn't a real person, and it was made up so no one had to sign their name." Bannon suggested.

"I kind of like the last one because it's the closest to the truth," said Haru." If we say he never made it or died, it could be an interesting story to share and imagine scenarios with his friends, or he may try to find people who knew him. We can't give him a mystery to solve or another secret to clutter up his head."

Gray nodded. He knew personally how irresistible a mystery could be to someone with a heightened sense of detail.

Haru reiterated, "Okay, so we'll tell him Alec T. was a secret name used by those in charge to keep them safe. He has proven he has the maturity for discretionary information. I'll tell him his grandfather was one of the people involved, and it's very confidential. That will appeal to his protective nature."

"Sounds good. Did anyone else see these papers? How about his dad, Henry?" Bannon asked, making sure the loose ends were neatly trimmed.

"No," Gray reported. "I spoke with Henry during his Hold interview, and he said he avoided looking at it. I think he's telling the truth. Everything about his demeanor said he was happy to be rid of everything on that shelf. He protectively never told his wife anything about the shelf, but of course, she knows what everyone else knows now."

"Connor, on the other hand," Haru continued, "smuggled souvenirs despite realizing how dangerous it was to know of them, let alone have them on his person. He's lucky he wasn't caught during the move."

"Hmm, he may be advanced in some ways, but he's still a kid, and he's dangerously territorial about what he deems as his." Gray pondered that for a moment. "I'll need to keep in touch with this kid. For now, he needs protection. He's close to Hannah and lives near Gabe. I'll have them keep an eye on him."

Just then, a knock came at the door. Haru got up and let Rand Lewis in to take his seat at the table. He was Bannon's technology expert. Within minutes another knock came, and Connor entered and took the seat he was silently offered. The eleven-year-old boy nervously sat with folded hands, visibly intimidated by the powerful men before him.

CHAPTER 1

A month had passed since my family and I arrived in New Haven. I thought back on the journey that brought me, my parents, and my little sister to our underground sanctuary in the Eisenhower Tunnel. It consisted of two parallel tunnels, each a mile and a third long. It was huge.

It was insulated from the Corporates because they believed it had fallen victim to a radiation accident a couple of years ago. It had been named the Poison Tunnel when news of the accident became public. In truth, it was a cleverly executed plan to keep the sanctuary town of New Haven safe and hidden from the Corporates.

The last four months swirled in my head like an impossible, terrifying dream. I experienced a lifetime of highs and lows in that short time. It started at our home in Denver when my grandad died. He was my best friend and mentor, and the only one who knew that I was a Highmind.

He taught me to keep my Highmind status private, and I still guard that secret. On the outside, it protected me from being taken to the camps. But now, having lived as this person for so long, I didn't feel comfortable letting people know the real me. I was born a Highmind, meaning I am genetically enhanced with various abilities. It was from an experiment my grandparents were involved in.

I don't know what it did to my grandad, but it gave me the ability to learn and solve complex problems at levels well above most geniuses. But the most dangerous ability was my eidetic memory. It meant I could remember everything I detected with my senses. I could even remember experiences from infancy.

I had to be careful to hide my intelligence to protect myself and everyone I knew. Hiding my true self would have been lonely, but I had my grandad. I didn't have to hide anything from him, but when he died, I found out he hid a lot from me.

Though it was forbidden to teach Dailys anything unrelated to their work, he educated me in all subjects, including history, which was especially dangerous. Even the Upper kids weren't taught history, but my grandad gave me lessons whenever we could find a safe time and place.

I called my grandad GD, and I thought I knew him completely. When he died, I snuck into his forbidden room to be near him. Going through his things, I learned he had dangerous connections with an underground rebel faction. It didn't take me long to figure out that upon discovering it, I instantly became an accomplice.

Although losing him was the hardest thing I had ever been through, I piled up several more losses during those summer months. We left GD's well-built house with all its secret fortifications and moved from one place to the next, shedding what few belongings we owned with each move. I thought my parents had lost their minds with each irrational decision they made. In my wildest dreams, I could not have imagined that a town liked this was the goal of that journey.

I climbed into the cart to go to the Town Hall building where Haru waited with the castle GD had built. The driver pulled into a well-lit alcove braced by four sturdy columns. A wall of windows revealed an open lobby that resembled the government building in Denver.

My dad and I traveled downtown to the Denver government building to register me when I turned nine. It was full of beautiful artwork and well-dressed Uppers walking around with tablets and papers. I could tell Dailys weren't welcome because we were quickly diverted away from the stunning lobby and into a dirty, crowded chamber with standing room only. New Haven's government building claimed to welcome all residents equally, but I had grave concerns about this meeting.

When I arrived at Town Hall, a Defender standing guard gestured me through the double doors and motioned me to sit and wait. I sat on one of the two tweed couches facing each other, flanked by small tables with colorful booklets on each. A long mahogany table separated them, sporting a serene lavender and white flower arrangement.

Ornately framed documents and paintings of men and women from a forgotten time lined the walls. I was tempted to investigate the reading material, but I didn't. Despite all that I had learned in the Hold about democracy, I felt that any minute now I would be led to the Daily room.

A woman ushered me up the stairs to a hall with photo after photo of New Haven's construction story. Stopping at one of the doors, she knocked, and I was led inside. The first thing I saw was the castle sitting in the middle of the table, which confirmed my fears that it was more than a puzzle.

The abrupt silence signaled that something important was being discussed before I entered. And though the men gathered around the long table smiled at me, it wasn't a glad-to-meet-you smile. It was a hungry smile. One that said they wanted something from me, and it was important enough for them all to be here when I delivered it.

I looked around the table, recognizing Haru and Gray, but two other men were unknown to me. It didn't take a genius to know that the dark-haired man with the blue eyes seated at the head of the table was important, and the tall curly-haired man with glasses to his right was important to him. I had assumed Haru and Gray were in charge, but I started to rethink that. These were all the town's leaders, and they were looking at me with keen anticipation. Worries began constricting my chest.

"Connor," Haru began and gestured to the man at the end of the table, "this is Bannon Vogel. He and his sister are the ones who set up this whole town. And this is Rand Lewis," pointing to the man on his right. "He is our technology and research expert. I want you to know you can trust everyone in this room."

Though I wasn't exactly sure what I was being asked to trust them with, I responded politely.

"I've been wanting to express my gratitude to you, Mr. Vogel. I love this town, and how you have helped us. We live in a safe, fair place where we aren't treated like Dailys. Thank you." It sounded rehearsed because it was. I wondered who had funded this monster of a project and planned to show my appreciation.

"It's my pleasure. I'm glad you appreciate it. I wish I could have done more. But this meeting is about how *you* can help us." Bannon was testing my declaration of appreciation.

"You want me to finish the castle," I answered, realizing there was more to this masterpiece than I initially believed.

I found it on GD's shelf when I snuck into his room. I hid it from my parents because I believed they would get rid of it. It was the kind of thing Dailys shouldn't have. But I just wanted something of his, so I could study it and solve its mysteries like we used to do. But now I was meeting with the town's top officials, and the sole topic was this castle. I had a feeling it wouldn't be mine for much longer.

I shared it with Hayden back in Denver because I thought it was just a puzzle. I know he's going to ask about it, but with this level of interest, I can't involve him. I am tired of keeping secrets and being afraid. I thought this place would eliminate the need for a life of subterfuge, but evidently not.

"Yes. As you know, your grandad helped hide many things for our town. We just want to make sure this is just a puzzle before we endanger you by having it. So, do you think you can finish it?" Bannon asked.

"Yeah, I only had one more step to go."

"How do you know that?" I could see Gray was invested in the mystery.

"It's the knight's creed my grandad taught me. A knight should be brave, true, wise, gracious, and skilled. B, for brave, so I figured it stood for the bridge. I had to be brave and stick my finger in the hole here." I pointed to the small cavity at the beginning of the bridge. "It punctured the tip of my finger, but nothing happened. So, I pressed down further, and spikes folded in on the sides, gripping my finger. That released the bridge. It left enough of a mark that I had to hide it from my mom. She's always worried about infections."

"You are something, kid," Gray said with admiration.

I smiled at the compliment and countered with my confession. "I tried using a pencil first, but it didn't work because it wasn't brave. When the bridge opened, it let my finger go, and I saw the compass rose decorating the floor inside. Every time I finished a step, there was a clue to the next one. T, for true, was for the tower. I turned the tallest turret to *true* north according to the floor compass.

"The next one, W, for wise, was hard, and it was tough to find alone time in the Hold to solve it. But I finally figured out a stenciled pane slid over the back window when the tower turned. I remembered something GD told me. Wisdom is the light that pulls the truth from darkness. So, I used the flashlight Officer Gray loaned me.

"When I shined it in the tower, a picture of a cross appeared, like the ones sticking up on the top of the tower. I pushed the cross down, and a bush at the bottom of the tower folded down and a knight flipped up. Then came G for the guard. I know knights graciously bowed before their king, so I bent him forward, and a tool popped up in the back. That's as far as I got."

"Wow, you want to come be my assistant sometime?" Rand asked with sincerity. "I'd love to train you on our high-tech computers. You'd enjoy the problems we get to solve."

I was excited by that idea, but Mr. Vogel glared at Rand. "Settle down, Rand. He's not working age yet. Okay Connor, go ahead."

I pushed the cross down, causing the knight to flip up. I bent the knight over in subjugation, and the tool popped up. Pulling it out, I saw Rand holding a finger up.

"Do you mind if I take a look at it?" Rand asked. He took a case from his front pocket and opened it. It was full of delicate tools and a small magnifying lens with a swing cover. Everyone watched with fascination and singular focus as Rand used the lens to inspect the castle.

"It's a mace from medieval times," he said as he pulled out the magnifying lens for a closer look. "The tip is arrow-shaped, and the handle has four fins, but they are oddly placed, making it impossible to hold in battle. There are miniature symbols painted on it."

He handed the mace and lens to me. It was in a code I knew well. I handed the lens back and said, "It says, 'Find the blade'." I thought for a minute. I doubted it referred to the sword. It was too obvious. The sword was in plain view, and no searching was required to see it. GD was never that transparent.

"Skill is the next word in the code, so the blade refers to the S for the sword, right?" Rand asked while handing the tool back to me.

"That's what I'm thinking," I lied. "I don't know how or where it fits. I also have to keep skill in mind, so I need to be patient and careful in how I go about it. May I borrow that?" I asked, pointing to the magnifying lens.

"Absolutely," Rand answered and handed me his lens. I was thorough and disciplined as they watched my every move with intense interest. I didn't allow myself to be rushed, though the previously unnoticed clock ticked loudly.

I examined the tool, the sword, and then the stone. I pulled back the bushy, tall grass behind the stone made of thin plastic filaments and found a green circular disk with a tiny slot. I examined the tool again. Not a tool, I observed, a key. Inserting the key, it sat upright in the slot. I pulled lightly on the sword. It remained steadfast. I tried gently turning it one way and then the other, but neither the sword nor the key budged.

I needed to think for a minute. I wondered if it could be tilted like a lever, so I pushed on it ever so gently. *Click*. The sword moved upward. Carefully and skillfully, I pulled the sword directly upward. It was attached to a thin scroll of rolled paper. I pulled slowly until the whole thing was removed. When it cleared the stone, the paper refurled itself into a coil. I was glad I had taken my time because if the scroll had become detached, it would have been lost in the castle grounds. There was no doubt in my mind that GD had a way to destroy the message if it was not retrieved correctly.

The whole crew of adults sat on the end of their seats with hands braced on the table's edges. They looked like vultures ready to pounce on the tiny blade and streamer. I eyed their over-interest and knew immediately this was the secret they were after. I wondered if my life would ever be free of dangerous secrets and whether it would be better not to know them.

Haru broke the intense mood. "It appears we have a new king." Everyone laughed. Even I saw the humor of the *sword-in-the-stone* reference, but like Arthur, I felt the weight of my situation swelling on my shoulders and my life filling up with ominous obligations.

"So, evidently not just a puzzle," I said to the team.

"I don't know, but we're crazy with curiosity. Do you mind?" Bannon held out his hand. But I didn't release the prize so quickly. I unfurled the note. Haru gave Bannon a side glance as I gave the tiny note a hard look, memorizing every strange symbol, number, and letter. There was also a coded message on the blade, which I quickly solved, said *Deliver to Tage*. "Who's Tage?" I asked.

Rand slowly raised his hand, hoping he hadn't over-stepped his place by divulging it. He looked at Bannon, and he nodded to continue. "That's my nickname. I'm gifted in the field of technology. I'm very good with electronic information, so people come to me like I'm a sage. Tech and sage together make Tage. But it's a term only a few people knew."

I wondered if gifted meant he was a Highmind like me. "Well, Tage," I turned to my left where Rand was seated, "this is for you. What do you make of it?" I handed the sword and the curled note to him.

He unrolled it with delicate precision, holding the tiny weapon and weighing the curled note down with the case of tools that sat in front of him. He raised the magnifying lens to his eye and began his examination. After several quiet minutes, he responded.

"I'd have to run it through my programs and work up a couple of theories. It will take some time to make more than a wild guess. First, I have to detach this message before we can return the sword to its stone." He went back to studying where the sword and message joined. Then, he pulled out a small razor from the tool case. Slowly and meticulously, he severed the scroll from the sword.

"If I give you the paper message, can I have the castle with the sword back?"

Bannon looked at Rand. "Well, I would like to check out the tool as well. But for the time being, the scroll and the tool are all I need," Rand said, answering Bannon's questioning look.

"I think that would be fine, at least for now," Bannon answered. "If we need your help again, can we count on you?"

"Yeah, that would be okay. I'm assuming I shouldn't talk about this, right?" I said as Rand slid the sword back into the stone with a click. The first thing that came to my mind was, what should I say to Hayden if he asked about the castle?

Bannon seemed to know what I was thinking and said, "Yeah, let's keep this on the down low for now. You don't have to keep the castle hidden, just don't advertise it or discuss the clues it provided." I nodded.

Gray then went on to explain Alec T. to me. He said the name Alec T. was a made-up name they used to keep the real people involved in this project safe. They asked me to discontinue my search for him and not repeat it to anyone. I assured them I had not and would keep the name safe.

It had not escaped my attention that Alec T. sounded like "elect" when read as one word. They told me that it was highly classified, but they didn't say what it stood for, and I didn't ask. There was a time when I might have been excited to know this kind of secret, but after the last few months, I've lost my desire to gather any more riddles.

Gray finished his instructions. "I hear you're good at holding things in confidence, so I think this information is safe with you. We are going to tell your parents we brought you here to pick up your castle and to thank you for your part in keeping the art safe. Can you live with that story?" Gray asked, looking directly at me.

"Yeah, it's pretty much what happened except for your looks that say a lot more is going on," I replied.

Bannon smiled and called for a cart to take me home. Within minutes, a Defender came to escort me and the box with my castle to the bus downstairs. I imagined the conversation going on now that I was out of the room. Although I was tired of being burdened with perilous information, I also knew my compulsion to unearth clues would return. It was in my nature.

CHAPTER 2

I cradled the box holding the castle my grandad made as I walked down the hall. My mind was in flux as I passed the windows that looked over the street of my new town. People were happily set on various pursuits unaware that our new little town was just as uncertain as those before the meteorites.

When I got downstairs, I saw the cart bus waiting to drive me home. Home, I have had a few of those this year. I sat at the back of the bus to avoid conversation and let my mind unravel. We moved from GD's fortified house in Denver to the town of Fairplay. There I adopted a dog, but it was taken from me. After a month, we were brought to a large warehouse where we lived in tents. It was called the Hold, and though we were not free to leave, we were treated kindly and well cared for. They gave us lessons on how to trust, began our formal education, and held activities in a recreation area. But it wasn't all pleasant.

I recalled how I trusted this new life, and I let my guard down. I asked a uniformed officer for help, something I would never have done before because it was dangerous. Next thing I knew, I was abducted and locked in a dark closet by a traitor Defender. It is a betrayal from which I still haven't recovered.

I believe the purpose of this place is to provide safety so freedom can flourish. Although most of the time this place feels secure, we just had an emergency lockdown. A woman was displaying signs of a serious illness, and she was trying to get away from the medical staff wanting to help her. We were told over an intercom system to stay inside, close our curtains, and not let anyone in.

It was proof that even here, where everyone was chosen based on thorough investigations, people are unpredictable and potentially hostile. And if that wasn't enough, the ugly world outside still loomed as large as ever. It would be foolish to think we won't be found.

As I rode through the town, I recalled the morning we left GD's house. I watched my home with the worn paint and the boarded-up window fade into the past as we pulled away. I thought no place would feel at home again. We built a lot of memories there, and leaving it was like losing my grandad all over again. GD had built a lot of advantages into that house before the meteorite strike ended the world he knew and loved, the world he shared with me.

The driver pulled up to 090, my new home. All the houses in this underground sanctuary had been designed by my grandad, and I imagined him secretly pouring over his creations. Every wall, window, and nook was saturated with his style, practical but elegant. This was as much his as that first house was, and I could feel his connection.

When I arrived home, I reeled in my worries. I took comfort in the knowledge that with every crisis, the Defenders brought us through with minimal issues. Yet, it was clear there were more secrets and dangerous mysteries to solve. The leaders of this town were thick into investigating... something, and it obviously had them worried.

I should have known it was too simple to believe it was just stolen artwork on a hidden shelf, just a puzzle, just a name, or just a dragon sculpture. Maybe baseball is more than just a game. I sighed. I needed GD to help me understand it all.

I felt a responsibility to continue investigating. The hidden answers and the looming threat demanded my attention. I justified my inaction saying it would be hard to access the information I would need. I was told to hand over my concerns, and they all but forbade me from looking into them myself. I wish I believed they could sort it all out without me. GD left me these clues, and he trained me to find and understand them. I think I'll start with his desk.

I walked in and my dog, Liberty, greeted me with energetic wags, and my little sister, Meshka, made a beeline for the box in my hands.

"What's in the box? Can I see?" she asked, holding out her hands, hoping I would let her take it. I didn't.

But her mop-top curls of gold are pretty hard to resist, so I told her to come to the table. My family crowded around the table. I wasn't sure how my mom was going to feel about me keeping it from her when her dad made it.

When I opened the box and removed the prize, it was met with oohs and aahs. I didn't demonstrate any of the mechanisms or explain the knight's creed, but the handmade castle was magnificent as a stationary item. I showed the interior of the keep through the still open draw bridge and pointed out the miniature features that I was thoroughly familiar with.

"I'm sorry I hid it, Mom. It was built by your dad. I should have shared it, but I was afraid you guys might think it was too dangerous to keep."

"You probably would have been right," my dad piped in with his eyebrow raised, "but let's just let that go. It's obvious it means something to the builders of this town to have a meeting about it, so it's good it was saved." My dad is smarter than he lets on.

My mom looked fondly at the structure before her. "My dad made me several toys as a child, but none were this intricate. I know he meant it for you because he told me he wanted to build you a castle full of secret nooks and crannies to satisfy your curious mind. You were only three when he said that."

I never knew that. The castle is far more than a mere novelty. It's steeped in treasonist secrets to help overthrow the Corporates. I questioned what happened when I was three to make him say that.

"Can I play with it?" asked the bounding six-year-old.

"No, this is not a toy," my dad jumped in. "Connor will hang on to it. Promise you won't touch it, Mesh." I could see he was questioning GD's judgment, and he didn't want his little girl anywhere near it. Would he have protected me if he knew what I was learning? Would I have wanted him to?

"Okay," she answered in a pouty voice that made me realize her lack of self-restraint meant I needed to find a secure place to keep it.

I went upstairs to my room, settled the box on the back of my high closet shelf, and went to sit on the balcony perched over our front door. Libby sat on her haunches faithfully by my side, staring through the railing.

I think she loved watching the people go by as much as I did. Their voices, bike chains, and scooter pushes created a rhythm of carefree bliss. The harmony was soon interrupted by the three rowdy voices of Teke, Hayden, and Kato.

"Condor! Let's play ball. We got you a scooter," yelled Hayden while Teke held up a baseball bat.

"Be down in a sec." I grabbed my mitt and hat and ran down yelling that I was going to the sports park. Two months ago, going outside my door alone was unthinkable. It was too dangerous. But now I just shout out my destination as I leave the house. How different my life is. I pushed away the new worries that the morning meeting had sprouted in my head. It was time to play baseball, and Libby and I were out the door instantly.

I had Libby on the leash as we rolled through the town, and she matched my speed with a smooth, choreographed stride. We stopped at the sports park that was next to the high school and parked our scooters. At 155 feet long and 45 feet wide, it was by far the largest field in the town, but it fell short of being big enough for an official baseball park. Lines were painted on the walls and back fence to mark foul balls, doubles, and home runs.

Mr. Vogel must have anticipated ball games being played here because the ceiling at this park was significantly taller than any other place in the tunnel. The lights at the top and on the sides were caged for protection, and the ceiling and walls were covered in shock-absorbing tiles instead of painted walls like the rest of the tunnel.

The rules of baseball and several other sports were adjusted to fit the available space. I looked up the New Haven sports regulations on my tablet. It explained that specially designed balls and bats were used to make the game challenging on the smaller field. The diamond area, though unmarked, was smaller than an official field, and the second base, shortstop, and centerfield positions were eliminated.

Gray says the rules may need further adjustment after a few games are played. I'm just glad we get to play, and I can't wait to get a couple of teams going. We just need twelve willing players to make two teams, and we can have a game.

We went to the shed and grabbed the catcher's mask and the four base plates. We walked off the modified distances for the bases and the pitcher's mound. I took off Libby's leash and filled her collapsable pet bowl with water from my canteen. As I tipped a drink for myself, she lapped greedily at the refreshment she craved after her run. Then she sat waiting for the order to retrieve the ball, as she had become accustomed to doing.

We played rock, paper, scissors to decide on the line-up for batter, pitcher, catcher, and fielder. I had been working with Teke and Kato on the art of throwing and catching, but this was everyone's first day at bat with this equipment. I went through some tips on stance and follow-through. I won the first at-bat, so I stepped up to home plate, took my stance, and sent my competitive stare down the firing line at Hayden.

He smiled, enjoying the silent banter, and he wound up to deliver his best heat.

"Hey, batter batter," Kato yelled from the outfield. Straight and true, it came right in the strike zone, and the ball whizzed past my frozen bat.

"Strike one!" yelled Teke through his pinched cheeks in the catcher's mask. All three burst out laughing. The teacher just got taught a lesson. I was anything but frustrated. The idea of stiff competition compelled me.

"Officer Gray told us to say that when you went to swing your bat," Kato said, still chuckling.

"Well," I said with a smile as I stepped back up to the plate. "It may have worked once, but I'm focused now."

Hayden just smirked and sunk another past my bat. "Strike two!" yelled Teke.

I stepped out of the box to adjust my shirt. It didn't need adjusting, but I did. This ball flew differently than my homemade one. I took a calming breath and stepped back in. Hayden lobbed a highball, and I let it through.

"Ball one!" Teke yelled.

Two more stinkers came my way. Whether they were intentional or failed attempts, I didn't fall for them. It was a full count, and he had to pitch to me now. He wound up, and I focused as the fastball came barreling toward me perfectly courting my bat. *Smack!* It was a heavenly sound as it hit the sweet spot, sending a bullet into the outfield.

The ball was designed to decrease its speed the further it went to accommodate the field size, but this ball bounced twice and still hit the back fence. I smiled. It was the best hit I had ever made. This equipment far exceeded the rag-sewn ball and rough-carved bat I used in Denver.

"That was awesome!" Hayden offered, and the other boys agreed.

We played through the line-up with each of us taking two turns before a group of teens came sporting an oblong ball. We gave them the field and decided to play with Libby on the sidelines while we watched this new sport we knew little about.

"Look how they spin that oblong ball to make it go straight," Kato observed.

"Is there a game with it, or is it just for playing catch?" Hayden responded. We watched the boys for several minutes in silence.

"Hey did you hear about the woman who held that girl hostage?" Kato asked as he teased Libby's head with his mitt.

"I heard she was sick and was afraid to be treated, but I didn't hear about a girl," I answered.

"Yeah, they live right next to me. The little girl seemed scared, and her mom acted nervous and twitched like a toxer. I saw her dragging her daughter down the street with a full backpack," Kato divulged.

Well, that was certainly a different story than the one I was told. I knew New Haven wasn't all sunshine and roses, but its dark side was getting darker by the day. Why would they let an addict become a resident? I don't know if I should be excited by the multiple mysteries to unravel or be questioning the town's integrity.

"It was weird how a speaker in the tunnel told us to stay inside and shut our curtains. I didn't know they could do that," Teke protested. Libby had happily settled herself in his lap while he scratched her ears and petted her coat.

"I understand that. I mean, if there is an emergency, they need to tell us what to do and where to go for safety. I imagine we will start having drills like we did in the Hold," I responded. "So hey, what happened to that girl and woman?"

"I don't know. Their house is quiet, like it's empty. I've seen the girl around. She goes to our school, but I haven't seen her mom."

The woman was probably in the hospital to address her addiction or whatever illness she had. And the girl was more than likely being cared for by others. Interesting. I tucked that info away and called Libby, seeing the four tall boys heading toward the equipment shed where we sat.

We decided to pack up and leave before they reached us. I guess we still didn't fully trust people we didn't know yet, especially bigger people. We hopped on our scooters and rode to the rec center to return what we borrowed. Defender Hannah was behind the counter and took our items.

I considered her a friend since she helped me when I was assaulted in the Hold.

After returning the equipment, we headed to the nearest dining hall to see if the sign-ups were still open. Residents were assigned to dining halls based on our schedule throughout the day. For instance, I am assigned to the Northwest dining hall closest to my home for most meals, and on school days I'm assigned to eat lunch at the Southwest one near my school. But if we want to eat with friends, we can sign in at a different diner. That way, food is allocated or moved without wasting precious resources.

I tied Libby to the rail outside and grabbed one of the water bowls set out for pets. They are very nice to pets here. I am required to take care of her, but they make it easy. Tonight, when I come for dinner, I will get yesterday's leftovers to feed her at the rail while we have dinner at a nearby table.

We signed in and checked out the menu on the tri-sided tablet display in the middle of the table. There are usually two to three main course choices, which change every day. Today we ordered mac'n'cheese with orange slices. We all pressed that option without even looking at the other choices. Soon a woman came rolling the cart with our lunches.

CHAPTER 3

I was sitting on my balcony waiting for my neighbor, Jilly. On Sundays, we walk Libby and talk about adjusting to New Haven. She smiled warmly up at me, and I sprinted downstairs with Libby to meet her. She wore a sage green sweater that highlighted her green eyes and contrasted the red hues in her hair. She had a cute face and a warm personality. I enjoyed her company, and we had the best conversations. Within a few minutes of walking, we were comparing our past lives to the New Haven lifestyle.

"It is a stark difference from the oppression we lived under as Dailys, but as awful as it could be, it was familiar," I stated as we watched a small girl keeping her balloon in the air with happy giggles.

"The rules were much simpler then: lie low and trust no one," Jilly said.

"Though the Corporate demons aren't physically breathing down our necks, they still torment our minds. All this freedom makes me nervous. I don't know how such a diverse community can work together without fighting," I responded. I enjoyed talking with Jilly because she took me seriously. I felt comfortable sharing my introspections out loud, and hearing them helped me understand and rethink them.

"Yeah, that's what the Corporates warned would happen if we didn't have strict rules. Everything ended with 'and then we would starve'," she laughed. "But Haru says we can fight with words and work toward solutions. I hope so," she sighed. She looked up at the large mint and slate blue hospital building with trepidation. I'm sure she is still assessing the attack at the Hold that sent her there.

"When I lived as a Daily, I had chores that occupied most of my day, and every night, I staggered with exhaustion down the hall to bed. Here, I have fewer chores and more time, but I get less done." She laughed when I said that, like it was true for her too.

"Maybe it's because our new responsibilities now require more thought," she said.

"Yeah, cooking and cleaning weren't complicated or interesting, but they're physically taxing. We had none of the modern conveniences we have here, so there was much to do."

"But you're not a worker anymore," she answered.

"I'm a student," I said. My noticeable pride made her smile.

"I know your grandad mentored you when he could, but I imagine you are beginning to tackle some pretty challenging lessons by now," she answered.

"Yeah, but even though my schoolwork is difficult, it's exciting to discover how all the subjects weave together. School and homework take a lot of time, but I still get to play baseball and hang out with friends," I replied. In my head, I added, and delve into GD's mysteries.

"But even my hobbies are challenging," I continued. "Baseball requires skills that take a lifetime to master. Friendships, I have found, are fraught with tiny misunderstandings that can expand into full-blown conspiracies. They are governed by a system of etiquette so complex that even if one is taught from infancy, there is little likelihood of mastery." I let out a slow, reverent breath, taking in the regrettable reality.

"Nothing could be more true," she answered. "Unlike family, there are no ties to force friends to continue a relationship. As Dailys, we spent all our off-work time with those in our households. We would fight and resolve it because we not only knew each other, we needed each other. We couldn't leave or move out without Corporate permission. We didn't engage with our co-workers. We just followed orders. None of us grew up learning how to navigate friendships because gathering together was forbidden. We were fully indoctrinated to mistrust everyone, especially those outside of our household.

"Every week, Haru sends lessons on communication and trust to our tablets. But we have both experienced violent betrayal while under the protection of this new democracy." She pursed her lips and let out a sigh as if she could blow her pain back into its box. "It's only natural we're holding back and being more polite than honest, which looks like deception. It's a lot to overcome, so don't be too hard on yourself," she said and smiled as if she realized the irony of her advice.

I restated this week's lesson. "Haru also says we need to be patient and give ourselves time to adjust. We see evidence that the goals of New Haven are fair and good. We just have to have faith that our beliefs will overcome our dysfunctions."

"It's clear we have a long journey before us. We will probably always be in a state of evaluating our relationships," she said with a thoughtful look, and I knew she was referring to Officer Gray.

We walked for a bit, enjoying the faux décor transforming into the emerging summer season. I knew our seasons were the opposite of those outside, and I reminded myself to research why.

Finally, I broke the silence. "I think our talks are very candid. I can't say I don't keep some secrets to myself, but I feel comfortable talking to you. You don't treat me like a child. With other people, I second guess myself all the time, but I trust you," I said.

We passed a dining hall, where we stopped to view the election posters. Within a couple of weeks, the New Haven residents over twenty-one would vote to elect two senators to represent the North and South town's people and a representative for each of the four sections of town.

I explained that at our school we were also electing representatives for our classes and a Senator from both schools. There are three schools, but the third one only goes up through Kindergarten. Our elections were to be held on the same day as the town's.

It was going to be a full weekend. The candidates were scheduled to present their ideas this Friday, and we had to give speeches about it. The Naming Ceremony was happening on Saturday, where we would find out the winners of the contest. Then, a fun event was planned at the big park. The election and Naming Ceremony conversations were a nice distraction, but before our walk ended, I had to ask.

"How about you and Gray? Any news there?" I looked apprehensively at him and adjusted my ball cap. This was a personal subject, but I knew them both reasonably well, and my interest was genuine. She and Officer Gray had begun a relationship at the Hold, and they both seemed so happy. Since the attack at the Hold on leaving day, she had pulled away from him. It was plain to see they both pined for each other.

"He kept secrets from me that I had a right to know." I liked Officer Gray, and I felt the need to defend him. Though her pain was evident, I jumped in before she could say more.

"I was closer to GD than anyone, and I was hurt when I discovered all the secrets he kept from me. His goal was to protect me, but he died unexpectedly and left me to figure it out. He never let on about any of it. It put me and my family in great danger," I emphasized. I knew she knew about the art items GD hid, but she didn't know there was so much more. "We all have secrets, old and ongoing. We hold them tight to keep the people we care about safe. Right or wrong, it's how we are wired."

"You are wise beyond your years, Connor. I suppose it will take some time to forgive and muddle through it. But... I will tell you this. Gray and I have a date tonight."

"I'm glad. I think you two make each other happy. You've seemed sad since you got here. Today your smile is back." I looked at her, and she was blushing. I was relieved that two people I cared about, and who clearly cared about each other, might be friends again.

We had arrived at our houses, and Ari, Jilly's sister, waved from her porch. Jilly and I said our goodbyes. I set Libby free in the backyard, where she bounded happily at being unleashed. Although our conversation ended, it continued in my head as I walked through the door. My dad was video chatting and laughing with a friend. He laughed often now.

I know secrets are the opposite of honesty, but they can also be a Pandora's Box of trouble. After meeting with the town heavyweights, I realized my days of keeping secrets were not over. We were secure from the world outside for now, but that wall was tenuous and bound to crumble. GD's training makes me involved ... in something. And that something is part of an elaborate plan to restore democracy.

Today is Monday, and the beginning of our third week of school since we arrived. The first few weeks were full of "fluff and stuff," as Gray called it because it involved introduction activities, more testing, and school procedures. This week we began our individual studies, or IS, based on our test scores.

Most mornings began with ninety minutes of IS and project work. We independently completed our assigned tasks at various stations around the room. Though we worked at different levels, our topics were similar. Throughout the room were colorful bulletin boards of information about our current studies and activities to experience the lessons.

Being able to learn with other kids was a fascinating novelty. Though school was a privilege, it helped that our teacher went around the room redirecting us. With that much freedom, conversations did stray to unrelated topics and even disagreements, but Miss Naddly said that acquiring the self-discipline to stay on task and get back on task were important lessons too. Miss Naddly was short, but she demanded respect while also being enthusiastic and inspiring.

Upper kids were also here, and although they had been able to attend school, it was fraught with bullies, cruel teachers, and bad information. Our teacher saw us as individuals and treated us with kindness and understanding. She told us we all have to unlearn what the Corporates taught us.

"In that way," she said, "we are all the same."

In the afternoon, everyone participated in activities, discussions, and videos. So far, I enjoyed literature and history the most, but science was getting more and more intriguing. Portable science stations were delivered, allowing us to engage in fascinating experiments. On Fridays after lunch, we worked on group projects while the teacher held focus lessons for those who needed them. I liked school, but it was definitely getting more difficult.

Art lessons were starting this week, and two afternoons a week would be devoted to them. I brought my Vadina pictures to show the art teacher, Miss Brooke, who also worked at the museum. I was a bit disappointed when she said we first had to learn the fundamentals of art. I had studied GD's sketchbook and learned to draw fairly well. However, I soon discovered his book lacked information regarding other mediums and the principles and techniques of color.

The next time she came, she brought oily chalks called pastels. I took one of my pen drawings out and began to fill in Vadina with color using the techniques she demonstrated. The black lines of the dragon on the white paper created a dramatic contrast, but the color brought her to life. It made me want to visit the museum again.

When I went home that night, I thought about the question I wanted to solve. *What do the marks on the base of Vadina mean?* In my head, I listed the places to search and people to talk to, like Alex Walker, the museum curator. I was deep in my thoughts when my mom called up the stairs.

"Connor, we're heading to dinner. Grab Libby on your way out."

"Okay," I yelled from my room.

I caught up to them near the dining hall, settled Libby on the rail, and grabbed a clean water bowl from the stack. We made our dinner choices on the tri-pad, and I also ordered pet food for Libby. I was deep in my head pondering my sleuthing plans when the food cart came our way. I grabbed Libby's bowl of food and walked it out to her. When I got back to the table, my mom gave me one of those concerned mom looks.

"I hope she has a better appetite than she did this morning. She hardly touched her food." Every morning, she took Meshka and Libby to breakfast where she caught the bus to school. She didn't have to be at work until late morning, so she would take Libby home before she went to her job at Town Hall.

I finished my meal and walked around the ivy-woven fence separating the street from the diner. Libby's bowl was still full. My mom was right. She hadn't eaten much of her food. While we were at the Hold, she hung out with the people at the ranch, and then with us before school and work. But now, she is left alone most days. She had a door to get out to the yard to do her business, but I had been getting reports of her barking as people passed by. I think she was lonely.

On the way home, I took a detour to find Officer Gray. Perhaps he had an idea of what I should do. I was heading toward the security building when I saw him walking.

"Hey, Officer Gray, can I talk to you for a minute?" he paused before entering the cornflower blue and ivory security building.

"What's up, Slugger?" Gray liked nicknames. I'm going to have to think up a couple for him.

"I think Libby is getting lonely during the day. She's losing her appetite and barking while we're gone. Since you took care of her for a while, I was wondering if you might have any ideas about how I can help her."

"Sure, how about I check in on her during the day? If I have time, I'll stop by and we can work with her on her barking. As far as her not eating, are you sure she's not sick?"

"She's full of energy every time I get home."

"Well, if I think she's ill, would you mind if I dropped her off at the ranch?"

"Will they help her? I mean, they won't … you know … think she's not worth saving."

"You need to take care of your garden dude, it's full of worry weeds. I assure you they will help her." I chuckled at his reference to my metaphor for concerns.

"Well, if she's sick, I want her to get better."

"Tell you what. I'll pick her up tomorrow and take her to Billie. I'm sure it's nothing."

"Thanks, GMan," I smiled. "I'll leave her outside," he chuckled at the nickname I used. I discovered law officers had once been called GMen, which was short for "government men". I turned to head back home, but I looked back and said, "I hope you and Jilly have a nice date tonight. You guys seemed happier when you were together."

"Oh, she told you, did she?" He turned abruptly and stood with his hands on his hips, head tilted, and his eyebrows raised.

"Yeah, she did, and she blushed," I replied with a smile. I pointed at him and said, "That means she likes you."

He flashed a big smile back and waved as he walked with a quick, confident stride to the double doors.

CHAPTER 4

This week at school we focused on government. We learned about the colonists, the Declaration of Independence, the Revolutionary War, and the United States Constitution. It was an overview delivered at a whirlwind pace to understand the hard-won value of self-governance. We were told more in-depth lessons on each of those historical events would occur over the next several years of our education, but this week Miss Naddly wanted to use the current elections to teach us about voting.

Part of me worried that all citizens, even angry or crazy ones, would be given the right to vote. Though NH's residents had been vetted before being allowed to join, I thought back to the traitor Defender at the Hold and the woman who caused the lockdown. I wasn't the only one who worried about trusting people with the town's welfare.

A girl in my class asked, "How can a government trust that every citizen cares about their community? What keeps them from voting for promises that only benefit themselves?"

"When the United States won its freedom, many of the kings and rulers of other countries believed it would fail for those very reasons. But self-governance is founded on the belief that most people are good-hearted and sane, and they want a fair government. With proper education, citizens can be taught to seek out various points of view and decide which ones they believe in. That's why we teach reading, writing, math, and all the other subjects needed to examine policies. If we only allowed the people we agreed with to vote, we'd be back to the world we just came from."

"Then why did the government fail?" asked someone else.

"There were many reasons, but the meteorite disaster played a significant role. You will spend years on the lessons of what went wrong, but today's objectives are about the work required of good citizens. Even after you graduate from school or college, you will still have homework because you need to study the issues and hold the government accountable. Throughout your schooling, you will learn how to determine if information is credible and how to recognize fair practices. It is everyone's responsibility to ensure democracy and liberty continue to thrive."

I was impressed with my classmates' questions and enjoyed the discussion. But when she said the word liberty, it triggered my attention to my dog. Although I called my dog Libby, her real name is Liberty. We couldn't say that word as Dailys without getting in trouble, so Mesh and I shortened it.

I was dozing into what-if land where Billie was examining my dog for illnesses, when my teacher began to explain our assignment.

"Your assignment for this week is to decide which race from your region you will cover. On Friday, you will watch the speeches of those candidates and decide who you would vote for. Next week, you will present your findings to the class."

We learned an excellent technique for taking notes called column notes. The template on our tablet displayed a table with three columns and a title box at the top. For this assignment, the columns were labeled *sub-topics*, *research*, and *conclusions*. We discussed what we thought the speakers should cover and added those to the sub-topics section of our templates. The other columns were where the notes on each sub-topic would go. This would work well to organize my mysteries too.

We also focused on speaking techniques and formats, and it was fascinating to discover how easily people could be fooled by such devices.

I never imagined that talking to people was so involved. I knew that divulging one's opinion could cause disagreements, but sharing opinions was a critical component of democracy. As interesting as the lesson was, my thoughts went back to Libby.

I ran all the way home, not wanting to wait for the bus. I was relieved to see Libby in the yard, and she jumped up on the fence when she saw me. I unlocked my front door with my keyband and charged inside. Libby met me as I opened the sliding door to the yard. I bent down and hugged her when I saw a note on the table.

Connor,

Libby has an intestinal infection. Billie believes she has been fighting it for a while. Several cases of this illness went undetected because the art of veterinary medicine was unpracticed for so long. She believes her illness is due to the starvation and scavenging most pets endured to survive.

She has made arrangements with the diner you are assigned to. They will be adding medicine to her food. This means she must only go to your assigned dining hall for the next five days until her treatment is finished.

Gray

P.S. You need to make Libby a follow-up appointment two weeks from now.

I still worried about all the time she was spending alone, yet I was glad she had medicine to get well. I promised to spend more time with her.

The week zoomed by, and along with the weekend came the candidates' speeches. My family and I went to our Northwest dining hall to watch with everyone else and see the town's reaction to the candidates. It was a brand-new concept and key to the democratic experience.

I carried a chair outside the fence to sit with Libby. She was eating better and had more energy. I was grateful for the medical help available, but I attributed some of her improvement to her having more attention from me, my family, and Officer Gray. She had two more days of medicine and a follow-up appointment next Monday. I hoped she would get a clean bill of health.

The town was separated into four sections, two on each tunnel. They were Northwest, Southwest, Northeast, and Southeast. Each section would elect a representative, and each tunnel would elect a senator. I decided to use the Senate race for my assignment, but I would watch all the candidates campaigning in my Northwest area. All the candidate's speeches would be shown on our tablets, screens, and the large portable screens at each dining hall. The representatives would speak in person at their respective dining halls after the senate speeches.

Two men were competing for the North Senator position, Carl Casberry and Vincent Jeffreys. The two men had used different speaking styles to attract a certain mindset. Though both assured the voters they had the town's best interests at heart, they went in opposite directions from there.

Casberry appealed to the former Dailys' decades of sacrifice. He enticed voters with plans to indulge them in recreational activities. Jeffreys petitioned the practical voter. He reminded them of how much work was still left to do. He was especially focused on education, and how we had fallen victim to its neglect during the decades of Corporate rule.

I remembered what Miss Naddly said about doing the work to be informed about issues and voting responsibly. Although Casberry's party time mantra sounded fun, it was all about the moment with little regard for forward progress.

Jeffrey's plan addressed the future and the hard work it would take to ensure our place in it. The choice was obvious, but I still needed to check out Jefferys's claims.

The next day was the Naming Ceremony, and it was going to be a big event. My teacher said it was a carnival with games, music, and sweet treats. I had never heard of a carnival, but it sounded amazing.

The big park's gates were pulled across the street, so the full width of the tunnel could be utilized. Small gaps were left open for foot traffic, but buses, bikes, and scooters were detoured through the three corridors.

Two weeks ago, residents were encouraged to send in suggestions to name the places in our town. I entered the Deegan Chance Maintenance Building. He had an integral part in the designing of this town, and the maintenance department brought that to fruition. The names were revealed before the games and refreshments at the tables opened up, and my suggestion won.

One name of interest to my friends and me was our school's name, Brad Anderson Middle School. He was a construction foreman who died while working on the schools. Others included James Madison High School, Wally's Rec Room, and our ballpark became Treagan Park. The museum was called the Samsara Museum, and the movie room, though not yet open, was named the Globe Theater. There were many other names, and the residents' love for the town grew stronger. Every day it felt more like the home I dreamed of.

After the names were announced, the activities opened up. My parents said I could go off with my friends, and I wove through the crowd gathering them up. We were so overwhelmed by all the choices, we just stood there for a moment looking around.

"Hey, I saw a game where you toss beanbags into holes cut in a board. It looks fun," said Teke.

"I want to try the bouncy net over there," interjected Hayden.

Kato just shook his head. "Look," he said as he pointed down the rows of tables to one loaded with every kind of cookie imaginable.

We made a dash to it and were allowed to choose two cookies. The woman behind the table said that if there were any left in two hours, we could come back for seconds. We used our bands to get our free treats and ran off.

We had to stand in line for the games, and it struck me there were a lot of kids here. Plenty for a couple of baseball teams. I left my friends at the tossing game and went to the table labeled Recreation Director, Carolyn Riddley. She was the one who talked to us when we first arrived.

"Miss Riddley?"

"Mrs. Riddley, how can I help you?"

"My name is Connor Wayther. I was wondering if you would help me organize a baseball club?"

"Baseball, huh?" she was smiling, a good sign. "How do you propose to go about that?"

"Well, first we would have to get people interested. Then we'd have to teach them the game," I answered.

"I like the idea, but I'm sorry to say it would be awhile before you could play a game. We have a lot yet to do to get this town fully up and running. We have many places unfinished and unopened. We are in the middle of our first election, and then there's the Winter Solstice. How about we plan to meet after that?"

I nodded because the decision was made. She saw my disappointment and offered me a compromise. "How about I put some baseball games and informative ads on the tablet's social page to begin drumming up that interest? When the Globe Theatre opens, we'll show a story about baseball. That will build more interest."

"That is a great idea. What movie do you have in mind?"

"Let me work on that. I'm not a baseball movie expert, but we have quite a selection of movies, and I'm sure we can find the perfect one."

"Since I'm trying to interest kids, at least at first, do you think there is one with kids playing baseball?"

"If there is, I'll find it. Connor Wayther," she said aloud as she typed my name into her tablet. "I'll send you word when I find something."

"Thanks, Mrs. Riddley," I said with a big grin. "I'll be looking for your email."

I caught back up with my friends at a baseball throwing game. Hannah, the defender who ran Wally's Rec Room, was working the stand. I looked over at Hayden, who had a small stuffed toy tiger tucked under his arm.

Teke and Kato had flat discs they said were for throwing. Hannah smiled at me and held up five baseballs.

"We won this stuff," Hayden said with excitement. "I'm giving this to Dace for the Winter Solstice," he added, feeling the need to explain the plush toy wasn't for himself. But I clued in on the idea of giving gifts. Dailys didn't give or get things because a day had a title. We struggled to get the things we needed.

I decided to try my skill at this baseball game. Maybe I could win a toy for Mesh. With the first throw, I hit within the strike zone, which earned me one point. The next one hit the zone too, but it missed the hole. To win the nice toys, I had to sink it through the center hole worth two points. It wasn't an accurate goal for pitching, but it demonstrated ball control. I focused and made the next two in the hole.

"That's six," Hannah yelled and pointed to the three boxes behind her. The first had *1-4*, the middle one *5-7*, and the far right one said *8-10*. It was my last ball, and I saw the toy I wanted in the top box. I took a cleansing breath and focused.

"Two!" Hannah and my friends shouted at once. I pointed to the striped kitten with shiny blue eyes.

"This will be a great Winter Solstice gift for your little sister," Hannah said as she handed me the stuffed pet.

Now, I just had to get it home without my snoopy little sister spoiling the surprise. When the event started winding down, I found my parents heading toward the gate. I stuffed her gift in my waistband, behind my back, and under my shirt, but my sister was so tired that there was no need to hide it. My dad had to carry her part of the way home.

CHAPTER 5

On Monday, I asked Miss Naddly if most student's educational progress was going well. Mr. Jefferys said it wasn't, and I wanted to see the evidence for myself and use it in my assignment. She confirmed his statement, and the score averages she showed me were alarming. I knew most kids weren't Highminds and their scores would be low, but I now worried we may never catch up enough to keep the town operating.

Remembering what GD said about being part of the solution, I offered to be a tutor two days a week after school. She said she would set me up with a student next week.

By Tuesday, we had all finished giving our speeches about the candidates we evaluated, and voting day was a week away. Now we focused on our school election. Only the grades above third were allowed to participate. That meant our school would have three representatives and one senator. The high school would have six reps, two senators, and a chairperson. Though each school would be limited to deciding its issues, group meetings may be held for special circumstances.

Only one kid, named Archie, accepted the nomination for class representative, but our teacher said we would still vote on the position because write-ins could alter the results. I nominated Hayden for Senator, and although Teke nominated me, I declined. My schedule was increasing, and my time was already stretched to the limit. Alicia was also nominated for senator. This was going to be an interesting race.

Posters for representatives were posted on our classroom walls. The school senator signs were pinned up at our school's dining hall next to the town posters. The school races caused as much excitement as the town races. Everyone was charged with "democrazy fever", as it was labeled.

The field trip to the New Haven Town Hall further enthralled us. I had been there before, but I couldn't talk about that. I was still excited because there were places I hadn't seen, like the Oval Room.

Through the double doors on the left side of the lobby, there was an ornate rounded room with beautifully elaborate leafy designs around the edge of its high domed ceiling. The backlighting played on the delicately decorated relief laced across the dome. A podium stood on a raised platform facing three rows of cushioned seats in a semi-circle.

Two long curved desks were flanked on either side of the podium, and each had four chairs. I knew they were for the mayor, the head of security, the four representatives, and the two senators. Off to the side was a lone desk for the secretary recording the minutes. I imagined standing at the podium and addressing the audience would be both validating and intimidating. It was a beautiful room, and I wished I could come watch one of the proceedings.

The town and the schools' vote were held on the same day. The adults had a seven-hour window to cast their votes, whereas we did it together in our classrooms. Hayden and Alicia each worked hard to persuade their classmates to vote their way. They both gave great speeches, and I had a hard time deciding who should win. Alicia spoke of a carnival event like Naming Day, only the focus would be science-based activities. Hayden promised to help create sports teams, starting with baseball. The lines were drawn, and the day came.

We were given paper ballots to fill out and put in a slotted box. At the end of the day, the votes were counted. After counting and recounting the three classes' votes, a tie was declared.

"What happens now?" I asked, wondering if there was a viable solution that didn't include doing the whole thing over.

"Well," the teacher paused, "believe it or not, most small elections that resulted in a tie were decided by a coin toss or some other game of chance. It was justified because half of the constituents would get who they voted for."

"I can't believe it. All that, and it comes down to gravity?" I said to the class.

"We could come up with our own solution. Does anyone have any ideas?" Miss Naddly offered.

"Just a minute," said Hayden. "Can Alicia, Archie, and I talk in private for a minute?"

They walked out of the classroom, and we all watched them through the windows, talking with hand gestures and thoughtful expressions. Then they came back in.

"I'm dropping out as class representative," said Archie. "I've been regretting accepting for a while now." I looked at the boy who had quit within minutes of winning. I expected to see some expression of disappointment, but he looked genuinely relieved by his decision.

"We have a proposal," Alicia said. "Hayden and I are willing to toss a coin, if anyone has such a thing, and the winner gets to be the Senator, and the loser gets to be the class Rep."

The teacher pulled out a small brown coin. She said it was her father's lucky penny, and she offered it for the finale.

Alicia chose tails, so Hayden got heads. Miss Naddly held it on the edge of her cupped fingers and flicked it with her thumb, sending it end over end in the air. She caught it and slapped it onto the back of her hand.

We were leaning over our seats waiting for the results. She lifted her hand and showed it to the competitors before she held up Alicia's hand.

"We have a winner!"

Everyone was cheering, and even Hayden had a smile. Awesome Day!

It was Monday, and I woke up an hour before my alarm. I had my reoccurring nightmare about crossing into Fairplay with the Denver Museum art book, GD's sketchbook, and the castle in my possession. But it was different this time.

The sketchbook fell out of my pack and onto the road. It opened up and started flapping like wings, and then it transformed into Vadina. She was an enormous creature, and she was angry. She was lifting off the ground, creating a fierce wind, and in her claws, she held GD's desk. Tons of papers were flying out of it straight into the hands of a Neighwah soldier with evil glowing eyes. He let out a maniacal laugh as he held the papers aloft. That's when I woke up.

Dreams are weird. GD thought it was our primitive subconscious minds trying to make sense of our experiences. Whenever I get these dreams, they point me toward the clues and mysteries he left behind. In the Hold, I was obsessed with learning to draw the dragon Vadina and solve the castle, and then I was taken and locked in a dark room. It took the wind out of my sails, and since then I have procrastinated restarting my investigation. I think my subconscious was telling me to get back to work.

I decided to re-look at the sketchbook. I had gone over every page and found nothing. GD had left notes all through it, and I read them, but I had not looked closely. I had given up because it was hard, but I needed to drill down into them and find what was under the surface.

I thought back on the days I had been twisted into knots by the dangerous secrets I carried, and worry permeated every aspect of my life. I was enjoying not having to live that way. I felt better. I slept better. I was happier. I hung out with my friends without wondering if I was putting them in danger. Haru assured me the adults would carry the burden of unraveling the dark world of espionage and soldiering, and I felt relieved.

But since that day in the conference room with the town leaders, I have felt unsettled. I don't have confidence that they can solve these questions without the knowledge my grandad taught me. I know they think I should not be involved because I'm a child. But the truth was they needed me. I was destined to uncover this... this big something.

GD taught me the lessons required, so, even if he wasn't around, I could recover... whatever he had hidden. I used to question some of the things he made me memorize. They had nothing to do with survival or academia. I thought he threw in that stuff to make learning mysterious and interesting, as if I needed more of that. The castle proved it was not random nonsense. That tool and that sword were clues to the next step.

The leaders of New Haven couldn't solve them, or they wouldn't have needed me to finish the castle. I wondered if they had solved the marks on the base of Vadina before they put her in the museum. They knew enough to cover them up so the public couldn't see them. I had a feeling they were connected to the castle. I recalled the decorative lines enhancing the bricks, plants, and other details of the castle had the same angled sway. Coincidence? Was anything GD did a coincidence?

Outside my window, the day lights began its transition to morning. The designers knew that being in the tunnel for years without the freedom to leave would cause people to physically long for the sun and sky. So, they recreated a day cycle with a sunrise, full day, and sunset. There were even soft storms with sudden streaks of lightning and low rumbles of thunder while a gentle rain cleared away the dust.

My window sat high on my bedroom wall and faced the edge of the tunnel. A series of colored lights positioned from the tunnel floor to our rooftop were scheduled to imitate the sun using a melody of colors throughout the day. I was sitting on my porch one evening when I noticed the pattern of lights fading in and out. I walked over to the wall and discovered it was coated with iridescent paint, creating a gentle glow on the walls of the tunnel. The curved ceiling eliminated the shadows, making the effect quite beautiful and soothing.

The sun lights were beginning to send a warm peach glow through my raised window. I still had an hour before I needed to get ready for school, so

I went to my desk and pulled out the sketchbook. I'm sure all these secrets are the key to the endurance of our town and the hopes of those still in the clutches of oppression.

Somehow, I will just have to prove they needed me. Between school, homework, the tutoring I would begin soon, and organizing a baseball club with kids who didn't know anything about the sport, I already had a very full plate.

GD never made his codes easy, and I knew this was going to take some time. I hoped it was time we had. I began my investigation using the three-column note technique I was taught during our government unit. But I did it on paper, so I could keep it from scans that could be performed on our tablets.

I wrote *sketchbook* and added the first subtopic heading, *page 7; "The lines need to be accurate like a map."* Next to it, I wrote *check maps* for similar line formations. I left the right side blank to add my efforts under this middle section and my results in the third. Thirty minutes quickly passed, and I heard my mom say she was taking Mesh and Libby to breakfast.

CHAPTER 6

I was still deep in thought about my new investigation when I noticed my tablet flashing. I had two messages. One was from my teacher. She had matched me with a student to tutor. Her name was Zoey, and I would meet with her on Tuesdays and Thursdays after school.

The other message was from Carol Riddley. She said she found the perfect movie, *The Rookie.* It is about a high school baseball coach and the team that inspired him to greatness. It was instructional, meaningful, and included kids, which we both agreed were important components.

She wanted me to watch the preview before she scheduled it. I sent her a note saying I could stop by after school today.

I told my friends I had to go watch a sample of a movie about baseball, and they begged to come with me. I was worried about showing up with three extras, but Mrs. Riddley was overjoyed. She showed us the three-minute preview, and we all loved it.

"So here's how it works," she said. "The movie theater will open three weeks before Winter Solstice, but all those movies will be about Christmas. That was a traditional religious holiday associated with what we now call Winter Solstice.

"For three weeks at a time, we will show two to three movies at various times. The first movie of each set is free, but watching more, and buying popcorn and drinks, costs credits. I think the movie house will be popular, and everyone will want to go, so you'll get a lot of coverage. How about I schedule it for the first set of movies in January?"

"Can people watch the movies on their tablets?" asked Kato.

Mrs. Riddley shook her head. "Haru says recreation is an opportunity to get people together, so it was decided a large percentage of the shows would only play in the Globe."

I recognized the theater name as the Renaissance stage where Shakespeare housed his plays so many centuries ago. I loved how our town had embraced the new while still giving homage to the old.

"So, what do we need to be ready for people wanting to join?" I asked getting back on track.

"It'll be advertised on everyone's tablet that the Globe Theatre is having its grand opening. At those shows, we will advertise the next set of movies, so people can make reservations. It is customary to show previews of future movies. Those previews will be shown on people's tablets too. I want you to do a short video speech about starting a baseball club. But before we can get this going, we must meet with the town leaders. That means you also need to get a presentation ready."

"I was hoping to have four teams at two levels, ten to thirteen-year-olds, and fourteen to eighteen-year-olds. But if the adults want a club too, that would be great. Since we have different rules for the smaller field, I only need seven players per team, which gives each team an extra, but more would be better."

Saying it out loud solidified in my mind how overwhelming the task was. How would I train them? I am not an expert player. I have never even played a real game. My heart was racing, and I felt I had caught myself in a trap of my own making. "I have a lot to do to be ready to organize and train teams."

My face must have revealed my apprehension. "Relax, Connor," Mrs. Riddley said in a soothing voice, "I'll see if I can't drum up some adult help after we get the okay. This kind of activity is new to all of us, but we have to start somewhere. It's the only way to make important things happen."

I was overjoyed that she called it important. I wasn't sure who she would find or how they could help, but I trusted her. Fascinating. Trusting people was becoming easier, just like Haru said. I decided to share my plans with him as soon as I had them shored up. This wouldn't leave time to work on the sketchbook or the desk. Vetting out buried secrets was a major objective, but so was reviving baseball. I hoped I wouldn't regret neglecting my search for GD's rebel stand to play a game, even if it did honor him.

As we left her office at the back of Wally's Rec Room, I turned to my cohorts. "Look, I'm feeling way over my head here. I need some help. Are you guys willing to put in some research time?" I said with a pleading tone in my voice.

Being the good friends they were, I gained three assistants. I delegated them to research the three aspects of the game. Kato took the game rules, Teke took the training schedules, and Hayden was on training techniques. I would focus on putting together a proposal for the Town Hall and writing the speech for the movie announcement.

I called this my big Monday because of all the commitments that I piled onto myself, including tutoring, which began tomorrow. "It's too much," I said softly to myself. "The tutoring job has to go, but I'll do it until a replacement can be found."

Tuesday came, and though I slept hard, I struggled to get up for school. We had been studying biology, and I remembered today was our field trip to the hospital. Since we began using microscopes, I had been curious to know what it was like. I got up quickly.

A nurse gave a tour of the patient rooms. He explained the equipment in each room and that there were two places for patients. One was the general ward, and the other was the isolation ward. Both could be used for any reason unless someone had a contagious illness. One patient was in the isolation ward getting ready for minor surgery to stitch up an injury, so we could only tour the general ward.

Each bed had equipment to monitor patients and assist the medical workers attending to them. It was the first time most of us had seen the inside of a hospital room, and it did a lot to calm our fears about them. Then he brought us to Dr. Maya's lab. It was the most interesting part of the excursion. The whole room was dedicated to diagnosing medical issues and developing medicines. Another room was full of various machines that could measure bodily functions and see inside a person. I was amazed at the capabilities available.

We were learning to write essays one paragraph at a time. On Thursday we were going to the ranches, and on Monday we'd be at the farms. Following each field trip, we will take time to discuss and write about what we learned from the experience. Our complete essay was due by the end of next week.

After school, I went to Zoey's classroom to meet her for tutoring. She sat with her hands folded on her desk. Fear radiated from a pair of soulful brown eyes peeking out from under her brunet bangs. Something bad had happened to her, but that described everyone. Yet she was still hiding from something, or she had a terrible secret she still couldn't tell. I didn't know which, but I understood both.

"So Zoey, I'm Connor. I'm going to help you with your schoolwork. What do you want to start with?"

She shrugged her shoulders in a painfully cautious and skittish manner.

"You know, Zoey, you aren't in trouble. Lots of kids need help with school. That's why other students like me are helping. I help my little sister too. Her name's Meshka. You probably know her."

Her eyes brightened a little, and she looked up at me. "I do know her. She's Savannah's friend, and they're in my class. Ellie is my friend, but she is in a different class even though I'm older."

"Well, Ellie had more schooling. That's what I'm going to help you with. Your teacher said that reading was the most important skill to focus on for now. How about we start with that?"

She smiled a slight, angelic smile and nodded her head. When the lesson was over, she had the "-at" word family nailed with all the consonants and blends.

"Are you going to come back?" she asked like her world was devoid of assurances.

"Yes, I'll be here after school every Tuesday and Thursday," I answered. How could I not? Either she was in some kind of trouble, or she thought she was. She needed a friend, someone she could trust. She had let me in, not completely, but it was a start, and I couldn't crush that.

One of the things I like best about New Haven is the freedom that comes from living in a safe society. In the Corporate world, we had cameras and patrols on watch, and New Haven is no different, but what is different is who is watching and why. Out there, we were watched to preserve Corporate control; in here, we're watched to keep everyone safe. The Corporates said they believed in our safety, but it was noticeably untrue. Dailys were sacrificed for minor transgressions, to demonstrate their control, or they were allowed to be abused without intervention. We were not safe, and they were the danger.

Here we can believe what we want, and more importantly, we can say what we want. We can go where we choose, well as long as it's within the tunnel, and we can feel completely safe even by ourselves. Somehow, I needed to assure this little girl of that.

Lately, I've been walking to school alone. I found it a beneficial time to organize my thoughts and plan my day. The walks also allowed me to appreciate the details added to this town for the sole purpose of making people feel content. The amount of attention paid to the smallest details never ceased to amaze me. They often had a benefit beyond aesthetics, like the rain showers.

This morning, a rain shower was scheduled for my tunnel section, and I wanted to see it. The rain, which came from the fire suppression sprinklers, served two purposes. It rinsed away the dust that built up on the surfaces, and it refreshed the air. But I would argue a third was to provide another beautiful display for people's enjoyment.

I sat on my porch waiting for the program to begin. A gentle streak of light shot across the ceiling further down the tunnel where the storm began. It was soon followed by a low growling rumble. It was so low that I had to listen carefully to hear it. The faint hiss of the sprinkler system followed, sending soft rainfall. Lightning and thunder moved down through the tunnel until it was directly overhead. The pattering rain and strobes of white bolts traveled past my home to complete the cycle, and after fifteen minutes, it was over.

The dew caught the peach hue of the sunrise lights, creating a world of precious pink gems winking from every surface. Large vases with tall, spiked plants and pots with flowers nestled on porches dripped onto the concrete streets, giving them a glassy sheen. Plastic chairs scattered in people's yards slowly emptied their puddles through their slotted seats.

Faithfully, they waited for the storm to pass, bicycles and scooters leaned under porches behind a curtain of dripping water. Vine-tangled fences dripped lazily in rhythm with the trees while small streams of water ran off rooftops and walls. Slowly the streams became trickles, then lingering droplets, and lastly the stillness and silence of a full morning sky.

CHAPTER 7

It was mid-November, so we were in the middle of our spring. Weird, I know, but a lot of psychology went into the decision to flip our seasons. When winter bites at the tunnel doors, the vents open and close to prevent their mechanisms from freezing. The intake system pumps fresh air through large underground tubes to absorb geothermal heat before being pumped into the tunnel.

With the geothermal influence, all the machinery, and the almost five hundred people plus livestock residing here, the tunnel is much warmer in the winter. In summer, when the vents are fully open, the air is pumped in directly, so it's cooler. To maintain the rhythm of our circadian physiology, inner clock, our seasons in the tunnel are opposite from what is happening outside.

It wasn't only our calendars that said so. The vegetation generously decorating every building and park echoed it. All the plants were manufactured to avoid the overwhelming maintenance, parasitical issues, and insect requirements, but it was hard to tell without close inspection. Credit-seeking teams of residents carried out the exchange of branches and other decor to imitate the seasons.

When we first arrived, the foliage was in its late winter phase. Sparsely adorned branches sported delicate leaf buds, and blossoms followed slowly, replacing the bare foliage with the fullness of spring.

I made my way to school. Remembering it was ranch day, I wore jeans and an older T-shirt. Billie led the tour, and I thanked her for taking care of Libby. She smiled, and as she turned her head, dark beaded braids cascaded around her shoulders. It was hard to ignore how pretty she was. We started with the chicken and rabbit side, and we even got to hold the baby rabbits and chicks while their pens were being cleaned.

I found the cleanout station impressive. They used rubber pellets that could be washed, rinsed, and spun in a big basin to be reused. The nutrient-rich rinse water was collected and used to water the farms. Each side had a small treatment section, but in between the farms was a more elaborate veterinary area. It pained me to know these animals had better medical care than the Dailys outside.

Our experience at the goat and pig ranch was the same, but their babies were much bigger and harder to handle. We were given leafy carrot ends to feed them and shown the open-hand method to avoid being bitten. Though we didn't get bitten, it caused a lot of the pieces to fall. A kid bent down to retrieve his carrot stub, and one of the larger young goats butted him. He was knocked forward into the clean pellet bin headfirst.

We all stood watching his feet kick about as he righted himself and climbed out. Pellets clung to his hair and shirt, and a shocked look covered his face. We were stunned and unsure how to respond. He looked okay, but we weren't certain if he would be in trouble. Billie hid the chuckles building up inside her, but the kid started laughing, causing the loose pellets to fall to the ground. The pellet sheds began to surround him, which made him laugh harder. He laughed so hard that he was holding his belly, making us all join in.

It always made for a fun day when we spent time outside the classroom. When our buses pulled up, Mrs. Naddly told us we were dismissed for the day. Before I went to meet Zoey at the school, I wanted to talk with my team about their research.

"I'll send you the training plan I found," said Kato. "It's a detailed plan from an organized ball club called Little League. Hayden says it has a lot of information on techniques too. It's all planned out, and we don't need to change it."

"Well," said Teke, "we *will* have to tweak some things. Our field is not regulation size, and neither are our rules, teams, or equipment, and we only have one field to play and practice on. But we can make it work."

"We should get some equipment and head to the ballpark today," Hayden added.

"I can't," I said with regret. "I have to tutor Zoey today, but it's only for half an hour. I'll meet you there."

"Hey, Connor, did you say Zoey?" asked Kato quietly as Teke and Hayden headed toward Wally's.

"Yeah, she's a first grader. She seems lost, and I don't think it's because of her schoolwork," I said.

Kato described the little girl he knew, confirming she was a person he knew. I suddenly regretted telling him about her, remembering what Miss Naddley had said about confidentiality.

"I'm sure she does feel lost," Kato added. "She was the one who was abducted when we had that lockdown." He had a flat-lipped look communicating both worry and anger about the situation.

"Did her mom ever come back? Are they back in their house?" I asked, feeling my detective nature kicking in.

"Nope," he said, with raised eyebrows and a tilt of his head. Then, he turned to catch up with Teke and Hayden.

"Hmm," I said quietly to myself. That explains a lot, but not enough. I tried to tamp down my curiosity about this poor little girl's situation. It wasn't my business, but I know what keeping scary secrets feels like.

It also seemed odd that the people of New Haven were left in the dark regarding a serious crime. I thought there were laws and courts that decided what happens to criminals. Who is Zoey living with now, and how is it that her mother lost custody without a whisper in the community?

I love a mystery, but this one could expose a tragedy that would hurt Zoey more than help her. It should probably stay hidden. I hoped Haru was taking care of her.

Zoey seemed less fearful and almost happy to see me. I was doing my best to stick to our assigned tasks, but there was one question I had to ask. I convinced myself it was reasonable and responsible to ask it, but I can't say I wasn't excited about the clues it might provide.

"Zoey, is there someone at home who can help you practice? It will be five days before we meet again, and I don't want you to lose ground." I even convinced myself it was a warranted question.

She told me she was living with a nice couple who were her guardians. She was tight-lipped and avoided any more conversation about it. Without further discussion, I added some work to her tablet.

Over the next four days, I worked up the baseball proposal based on the research the team provided me. I showed it to Carol Riddely, and she made an appointment for me to present it to the city leaders on Wednesday. She said our plan was well thought out. She also said she wouldn't be able to make the meeting. I was ready, so I decided to worry about that later.

After seeing Mrs. Riddely, I met my friends to play baseball. We caught the interest of some high schoolers as they passed us on their way to the basketball courts at our school's park.

"Is that baseball that you guys are playing?" asked the tall kid with short brown hair and big dark eyes.

"Yeah," we said almost in unison.

"How do you guys know about baseball? I know we all learned about basketball in the Hold, but baseball, that's like a myth," said a stocky kid wearing a sports jersey.

"My grandad taught me in secret. I'm not an expert. I mean, I've never even played a game because gathering for that sort of thing wasn't possible.

But my grandad played in high school and college," I answered while my friends looked on.

"Well, can you show us how to play?" asked another. "I'm Noah, and this is Walker, Dan, and Jade." I quickly locked their faces to their names. This could be the start of the high school team. Noah was the dark-eyed kid, Walker was a green-eyed blonde, Dan was the stocky one, and Jade was the brunette girl with chocolate-brown eyes. She looked too young for high school, but seventh graders went there too, and I assumed she was one of them.

"Absolutely," I responded, trying to reel in my enthusiasm.

After a brief description of catching and throwing techniques, we threw the ball around for a while taking turns with the mitts. They naturally struggled at first, but soon we were having fun. We agreed to meet again tomorrow after my tutoring lesson. With this kind of interest, I knew I would get a ball club going, and we were one step closer to playing a real game. My excitement soared through the pretend sky and into the real one.

All day at school, I was looking forward to playing baseball with our new friends. I tried to focus on Zoey's lessons, but she noticed I was distracted.

"Are you mad about something?" she asked.

I smiled at her. "Not in the least," I said. "I am excited about playing baseball. I'm sorry, it's got me sidetracked a bit. I'll do better."

"I get it," she said. "Music is like that to me. I hear music in everything." She had a whimsical, dreamy look as she continued. "I used to sing and dance with my real mom before my aunt ..." she said the word aunt with resentment and then stopped suddenly with a horrified look on her face. There it was, that big scary secret eating away at her. I was already creating a tri-column note in my head. *Title: Mom versus Aunt; subtopic one: What happened to real mom? (remembered fondly); subtopic two: how did Zoey's aunt get here with her? (not fond of); subtopic three: What was she going to force Zoey to do?*

I put my hand on her shoulder. "You know, I bet we could use music in some of our lessons. Would you like that?" She nodded, and we continued the rest of our time without mentioning the unmentionable.

The high schoolers returned, and we introduced batting practice. All of us were experiencing the learning curve. Hitting a baseball is hard enough with years of practice, which none of us had. And although these balls weren't regulation baseballs, we didn't know the difference.

The tunnel balls could be thrown fast, but when the specially designed bats hit one, it triggered a reaction in the ball that slowed it down while increasing its spin and trajectory. It was designed to make playing the game competitive and exciting in the field available.

Wednesday arrived, and I felt I had practiced my proposal enough for the presentation. I made diagrams, took pictures of the field, made lists of necessary equipment, and outlined a timeline for each task. I walked down the street knowing I was prepared, but the closer I got to City Hall, the more I felt the creeping vines of doubt. They snaked through my confidence, squeezing the life out of my plan.

Walking through the lobby, a lady met me and directed me to the chairs upstairs, seated against a wall of windows. They faced a row of doors where the heart of our city beat out the rhythm of the people pumping through our streets. I couldn't relax, so I stood looking down at the people below.

None of them knew I was here or what I was trying to do. I think from this day forward I will wonder what decisions are being conjured and discussed as I walk by.

Waiting is the worst part of being in the present. It messes with time and swirls what-ifs through one's head. The longer I sat there, the more my confidence faded. When I was summoned into the conference room, I walked with all the assurance my shaking legs could allow.

"Good afternoon, Connor," said Haru. "I hear you have something to tell us."

I froze for a couple of seconds. Did they know Zoey confided in me? Or were they searching for more secrets? Gray broke the heavy silence.

"I heard it's about starting a baseball club. Sounds like a good idea." He had on his detective look like he was dissecting my thoughts.

I handed Haru my tablet, and he linked it to the center console that rose from the table. I took a breath and began my spiel.

"I think we should have some organized sports clubs to keep kids busy with more than school. There is a lot to do here, but learning a physical skill and being part of a team are healthy endeavors." All three of them looked at me with such intent that I almost wished they would slouch in their chairs. Breaking eye contact with them, I pulled up my first visuals.

I showed pictures of school sports at several levels from a time before the world fell apart. They never interrupted me, so I had no idea what they were thinking.

"This is a picture I took Monday. Four high schoolers saw us playing catch and asked to join in. Kids are drawn to physical activity with others. We like competition, and we want to play organized sports like kids used to. Other kids have asked to join, but my dad said I should get your approval before I caused a political problem."

Mr. Vogel smiled at my last statement and spoke first. "It has always been our intention to have organized sports. We just aren't ready yet. There are a lot of places in our town that are unfinished and unopened, and some tasks require immediate attention. But if I get the direction of your proposal, you are willing to take this on. I just have a few questions, Connor. Have you ever played a game of baseball?" Gray gave Mr. Vogel a hard look, but I wasn't sure why.

"No, that was impossible. My granddad played in high school and a year in college before sports were canceled. He taught me a lot about baseball. I know I'm winging it here, but I think it's important, and somebody has to start it. Kids get restless if they don't have something structured and exciting to belong to."

"I agree with you, Connor," said Haru.

"Do you have a plan for how you will accomplish this?" asked Gray.

I failed to grasp what hung in the air between Mr. Vogel and Officer Gray, but I proceeded to present my timeline, Little League plan, and my requests for supplies. I described what I thought would be a workable practice and game schedule, and that the goal would be to form four teams at two levels and proceed from there as interest dictates.

"I'm going to work on this, Connor. I will help you make this happen, but we need time. Are you okay with that?" Mr Vogel asked.

I nodded because it was the only response possible. I wish I could have heard the conversation that proceeded after I closed the door. They didn't say no, but it was definitely a not now.

I knew my timeline, but theirs was a mystery. I was still determined, but I could feel my shoulders droop just enough that I needed to reboot my enthusiasm. The best way to do that was to be with my friends and play some baseball.

CHAPTER 8

It was a Wednesday, and a week had passed since I presented my plan to City Hall. I had heard nothing from them. They had pushed my idea to the wayside while they dealt with more pressing tasks. I wondered if they even liked baseball. I know God didn't send me here to restore baseball, but I asked Him to help me anyway. I hope He likes baseball.

Maybe those tasks the leaders were busy with had to do with finding what the castle scroll was hiding. That *would* be more pressing, and it should be my focus too, but right now, those mysteries had stiff competition. Several more kids joined us and learned the basics of baseball. We had enough for a game, so for now, baseball won.

"We have fourteen people, Connor," stressed Noah. "Let's have a real game and invite people to watch. We need to play to learn, and the town needs to see why we need to have a ball club."

"I agree," added Jade. "It's time we took this to the next level."

I sighed. "We'd need an umpire and permission to close the street, but the town leaders said to wait, and I gave them my word." I didn't mean to drain the enthusiasm building among the players. I was hesitant because if the leaders wanted to, they could rip the whole plan out from under us.

"Good grief, Connor. Stop overthinking it," Hayden stated with restrained frustration. "Let's just play a game."

I sighed. Hayden was right. We were all done with politics worming into our pastime. There was no reason we couldn't play a game. Why would it be wrong if a few people came to watch? "Okay, what Saturday can everyone meet for a game?" We settled on the second Saturday of December. That was just over a week away.

Since this plan required sliding the gates closed, it meant getting permission and giving notice of when traffic would be diverted to the corridors. Mrs. Riddley granted permission, thinking, as I did, that it was a small game. I was relieved I didn't need to go back to City Hall.

The word got out, and parents and friends started lining up to attend. It was turning into a crowd, and I wondered how many could squish in front of the gates. One of the kids told his dad, who was a manager at the maintenance shop, about the growing crowd of residents. His dad said that made it a safety issue, so he was able to get four sets of bleachers from storage and modify them to fit.

Next thing I knew, the diners committed to popping corn for the spectators. Two high school students studying journalism said they would film the game, and their teacher said he'd put it on a live stream. Great, I thought. Now, resources were being spent. This is what my dad meant when he told me not to make political trouble. We didn't mean to go over anyone's head; we just wanted to play a game, but it took on a life of its own.

I invited Zoey, and she told me another piece of her puzzle, which threw me an additional curveball.

"I told Dana and Indy, my guardians, about the game. Indy says he wants to talk to you."

"Okay," I said with apprehension.

"Oh, it's not anything bad. He likes how you've been helping me. Dana is Bannon's sister, and they helped make this town," she said with pride.

My stomach lurched. The town mayor's sister and her husband had somehow acquired the little girl of someone who had ruffled the political nest. And now, I too had ruffled this nest. This whole thing was blowing up in my face. I didn't think I would disappear, I hoped, but it would serve me right if I had to call the whole thing off and apologize to the town as a lesson to all.

I fought to maintain my cool during the rest of our lesson. I was being pulled in every direction by strangling worry. I contemplated telling the teams before the verdict was slapped on me. I had no idea what the future held for our game or our ball club, but I owed it to everyone to try to salvage it. I needed to talk to Haru.

Our lesson was almost finished when a man walked into the classroom. He was tall with curly reddish-brown hair. He looked distinguished in his blazer and jeans, and I wondered what he wanted.

"You must be Connor," he said, with his hand out. "I'm Indy, Zoey's… guardian."

Well, so much for talking with Haru first. I recovered from my stunned look, took on a professional posture, and readied myself to report Zoey's progress. Hayden and his two younger siblings used to come to our Denver house, and we co-babysat while our parents worked. At the end of each day when his stepmom picked them up, I would give her a daily report. I was thankful for that practice because my nerves were too raw to compose myself without a familiar format to follow.

"She's a good student. It's been my pleasure to work with her." I stood up, and we shook hands. He had a firm and commanding grip.

"I've heard good things about you from Zoey. We are all happy with her progress."

I gave the short version of Zoey's progress report and waited for the topic electrifying the air like the tingle before a lightning strike. I was hoping to work out my quagmire with Haru before hashing it out with a stranger. And not just any stranger, but one who was related to the founder and mayor of our town.

"So, I hear you are trying to form a ball club."

Snap! There it was. I took a long breath, waiting for the rumble of a scolding. "Look, I can explain…"

He interrupted me, saying, "I used to coach high school baseball. I was wondering if I could help."

My attempt to portray a calm and confident attitude was betrayed as a wave of shock rocked through me. This was worse than the berating I expected and deserved. He either had no idea that everything was unsanctioned, or he didn't care. I desperately needed the very assistance he offered, but that meant another person was involved with my non-sanctioned project, and not just any person, the mayor's brother-in-law.

Indy responded to my distress with an apology. "I'm sorry. I don't mean to take over. I just wanted to be a part of a team again."

"That's not it Mr. Indy, sir. I would normally be jumping for joy at your coaching expertise. I am so over my head. It's just this whole thing has taken on a life of its own, and I'm afraid Mr. Vogel is going to be mad and pull the plug. He asked me to wait, and I planned to. All we wanted to do was play a game and invite a few people to watch. I never expected so many people to want in on it." I told him all about the add-ons since the word got out.

He started laughing. "Oh, man. That's hilarious. You definitely got the snowball effect going." He continued chuckling and shaking his head, enjoying the fiasco at my expense. He looked up and must have seen my distress. "How about this? Turn the coaching over to me, and I'll shore up this runaway train. Relax, Connor. It's going to be okay. The Bannon I know isn't going to be angry or let the town down when they are excited about something positive. It's more likely he'll want front-row seats to New Haven's first ballgame."

"He can have them," I said. I could feel my posture ease and my shoulders unwind as relief started to untangle my state. I could even feel my enthusiasm returning.

I'm not sure what Indy said, but the next thing I knew I had messages on my tablet from Gray, Mr. Vogel, and Haru. They all said they wanted to meet with me to finalize the plans for the baseball game. Indy said he'd come with me.

Indy showed up at our practices, mostly to see what we knew. Though he offered advice here and there, the biggest change he made was shortening the game to five innings for all but the adult teams. He said it would help with the crowded schedule on the one field, and we could use more time to build up our arms and improve our techniques, so we wouldn't injure ourselves. This was especially true for the pitchers.

Before it was all said and done, raised bleachers were being erected behind the street gates, and netted dugouts with bullpens were being fashioned behind both sides of home plate. Maintenance crews worked round the clock to install everything that Friday before the game Saturday afternoon.

Game day was finally here, and I made my way to the park. People waved with good luck wishes and promises to watch. It surprised me that so many people knew who I was.

I arrived at the park in time to see the portable bleachers unfolding at each end of the field. The dugout nets were attached to the gates, with benches placed below the bleachers. Carolyn Riddley and Hannah pulled up with a cart full of equipment, and the team went to help unload it.

"So, you must be over the moon excited," Hannah said to me.

I gave her a shrug and smiled. "Actually," I said, "I'm a little worried that we are going to be a disappointment. I've watched numerous professional baseball games, and those players were amazing. I've heard many people have also been watching Major League games in anticipation of this day, but they have been watching professionals. We aren't even worthy enough to be called amateurs."

"I think you missed the point. They aren't coming to see expert players. They are coming to see something new and fun that belongs to our town. It's not yours anymore, Connor. It belongs to all of us. Just play ball, and stop overthinking it," she smiled.

"I'm told that a lot," I laughed.

The teams showed up and took turns throwing the ball around to warm up. Vests were issued to distinguish the two teams. The crowd began to fill the four bleachers, which I learned could hold forty spectators each. That's one hundred and sixty people plus those watching from their homes. Before the game started, every space was filled. Many children sat on adults' laps, and more sat on chairs behind the outfield.

I motioned Mr. Vogel to come through the gate and onto the field. Noah used the microphone to speak for the players.

"It is tradition that the first pitch be delivered by someone we want to honor. We voted, and we would like to give this honor to you, Mr. Vogel, for setting up this town and making us free."

Everyone rose from their seats as cheers reverberated through the crowd. The stunned and humbled man positioned himself on the mound, wound up, and delivered a nice fastball to the catcher's mitt. I was impressed.

Indy was the head umpire. He made his way to home plate and called the teams to line up in front of their dugouts. A young man walked to the middle of the field holding a microphone. A voice boomed from the speakers, asking everyone to stand and face the red and white striped flag with a single star on a field of blue.

I knew to put my right hand on my heart, and I saw a few others do it too. Pretty soon, most had imitated the gesture, and a melody filled the air. The young man sang a song about a flag still flying after an intense battle. It symbolized to its followers that they were victorious. The lyrics ended with a crescendo of "for the land of the free and the home of the brave." Praises and clapping rumbled from the audience.

Play ball!" yelled Indy as he took his position. My team was the home team, so we ran out onto the field while the visiting team waited behind in their dugout. Gray had been studying the rules and volunteered to officiate the outfield. Dan, one of the high school kids from just a few weeks ago, took his place on the mound, and Hayden came out as the lead-off batter.

Dan looked at me, the catcher, and I gave him the sign for a fastball. It whizzed past Hayden.

"Strike one!" Indy yelled with a chop of his hand. The audience sat unsure whether to clap, cheer, or remain silent. My team shouted with enthusiasm, causing the crowd to join in.

"Strike two!" This time the watchers cheered in without our lead.

Hayden dug in. He looked surprisingly focused. I signaled for a change-up. *SWACK*! Up it went, and Hayden shot for first base. Our outfielder didn't get under it, and Hayden made it to second.

"Safe!" Gray said with a two-handed sweeping gesture. The crowd was on their feet yelling and whistling.

Dan struck out the next two batters with ease, but the next hitter was Noah. Noah was good, and I paused the game and walked to the mound to rally Dan's confidence.

"Send him a couple of fastballs and then hit him with that curveball we've been practicing in secret," I told him, and he gave me a nod.

"Foul ball," came the first call. Then it was followed by another, but when Dan sent the curveball, Noah hit it. It wasn't foul, but it was wonky, causing the outfield to scramble. Hayden made it home, but Noah was tagged at second. Our turn.

I discovered the fans were cheering for every win regardless of which side achieved it. They had never attended an event like this, and they were enjoying the excitement. I too, enjoyed every well-made play regardless of which team executed it. I could tell the players, me included, found it exhilarating to play before a cheering crowd because we all performed better than we ever had.

It was the top of the fifth, the last inning, and the score was tied. It was my turn to pitch. We had two outs, and the bases were empty. Hayden stood before me with a confidently charged grin. The count was two strikes and two balls. I signaled to the catcher I was delivering a change-up.

"Foul ball!" shouted Indy.

The next pitch delivered a full count. I signaled the catcher again, this time for a curveball. I wound up and gave it a beautiful spin, but Hayden's bat made solid contact. It soared until it hit above the home run line on the far wall. It was the first home run ever in New Haven, and the crowd reacted with elation

It was our last at-bat. Visitors four, our team three. We needed two runs. The first batter got out on a fly ball to left field. The second batter got a walk and stole second on an overthrow. Our third player struck out. We had two outs, and I was up to bat. If I could send the runner on second to home, that would tie it up, giving us an extra inning, but I was going for more. I stared down the field at the other team's best pitcher, Noah. The first two throws were balls, but our runner stole third. The next pitch swished past me.

"Strike one!"

Two and one, the hitter's count. I could choose, but the pitcher had to throw a strike.

"Foul ball!"

The count was two and two. I focused. This was the one. I could feel it. It was a beautiful change-up, but my bat hit it fat and true. *Smack!* I watched it slap against the home run section! The crowd roared with excitement.

"That's a win for the home team!" shouted the announcer.

Gray came in from the outfield and slapped me on the back. "Killer game, kid."

"Thanks, Blue," I said using an old slang term for umpires. He smiled and headed to the dugout to start gathering the equipment.

I walked over to Indy. "Good job today, Sir."

"You too," he said, smiling and patting my back.

It was the best day ever, and the still-rumbling crowd agreed. Both teams shook hands, and smiles permeated every face. Requests were shouted from behind the gate by kids and adults wanting to join the ball club. We successfully stirred up some interest, maybe too much.

I thought back to the simple plan three weeks ago, wondering if we could find enough people to play. Back in Denver, at GD's house, we used to steal away to play ball, hoping we wouldn't get caught. It was a hard and unfair life, but it was predictable, and I accepted it. Now, I live in my dream world where everything changes, few outcomes are predictable, and though I don't always agree with it, I love it.

Each change brings something worth having, even if it's just the experience of getting through it. I am thankful, and I see changes as opportunities where I can strive to be more. If freedom is being allowed to think for ourselves, choose our passions and directions, to live our lives as we see fit, I feel free.

So far, despite my doubts, every change has made life better. I wonder if that's how freedom works, or is it luck? I hope it's the first one because the one thing I know about luck is; it runs out.

CHAPTER 9

When December arrived, it came with snow-flocked pine trees scattered among the summer decor. They were adorned with sparkling bobbles, and colorful lights were swirled around them. At the schools, only the lights were on the trees, so the students could finish decorating them. We made ornaments during craft time and hung them on the tree in front of our school. I was amused that several resembled baseballs.

Sunsets were scheduled an hour earlier to honor the Winter Solstice and to allow time to enjoy the illuminated decorations. And though they contrasted the emerging summer embellishments, everyone was enthralled to see the festive traditional décor. In honor of the event, we studied the revolution and orbit of the Earth as well as the various beliefs surrounding the darkest day of the year. The concepts of our galaxy and the universe were new to us.

Under the Corporates, the Uppers were allowed to celebrate holidays, but the closest Dailys came to the festivities was working to make them happen and watching their betters enjoy them. But everyone was included now, and I had never seen so many joyful people.

A town market was scheduled for the following weekend, allowing residents to sell homemade items for credits. Credits were earned by volunteering and now, trading goods and services. I had a nice account from tutoring, setting up the first ball game, and helping plan the baseball club starting in January.

With our credits, we could buy gifts for our family and friends. I already had a present for Mesh. For my friends' gifts, I set it up with Mrs. Riddely that we would get snacks for the baseball movie scheduled in January. I purchased a pack of canvas paper and borrowed art supplies from school to make gifts for my adult friends. I just needed to find some stuff for my parents.

The market had lots of home-crafted items. Jillian made soaps with heavenly fragrances. I bought my dad three pine-scented ones, and I got my mom flowers for her empty table. It was a bouquet of pink, white, and lavender flowers with gentle sage foliage perfectly arranged in a white ceramic vase. It cost me a lot of credits, but I knew she would love it.

The same games at the Naming Ceremony were set up, and I used the rest of my credits on them. I won a small giraffe for Zoey and a ball for Libby.

Winter Solstice was officially on a Thursday, but because everyone couldn't be off at the same time, it was celebrated over three days. On my family's day, no one in our household worked or went to school.

My family's day was Wednesday, so I decided to hand out my artwork gifts on Tuesday as I walked home from school. I created Miss Naddly a street view of New Haven Town Hall. Mrs. Riddley and Hannah received a large colorful collage of sports equipment. They hung it behind the counter at Wally's. It was next to the photos of our teams, under a plaque titled *New Haven's First Baseball Teams*. I hoped more would follow.

I painted Ari and Jilly a picture of a boat with taut sails leaning into the wind, and they gave me a new collar for Libby. For Haru, I painted blue-green waves crashing on a sunny beach, and he gave me a box with all kinds of art supplies. Officer Gray's picture was of a motorcycle riding through a winding mountain road lush with tall pines, and he gave me a flashlight. This gift-giving business was fun, but it still seemed odd and had the potential to get expensive.

Gray showed me the engagement ring he was giving to Jilly. Jilly told me she was giving him a guitar because his was destroyed. I should be happy for them, and mostly I was. Yet, I couldn't help but think that if she said yes, I would lose my neighbors because Ari was already engaged to Mr. Vogel, and they said they planned to move into their husbands' homes. Both couples should be together, but I didn't want to lose my neighbors or give up our Sunday walks.

Our family's celebration day arrived, and we started it by going to breakfast. I had waffles with maple syrup, applesauce, and bacon. When we came home, it was finally time to exchange presents. I found I was more excited to give gifts than get them. I gave Libby the ball I won, then I turned to Mesh.

"This is for you," I smiled and held out her gift. She reached for it and pulled the plush striped kitten to her. Happiness radiated from her as she took it in her arms and came over and hugged me.

"Thank you, Connor." She was snuggling the blue-eyed pet as if it were a long-lost friend. "I'm going to name her… umm… Kiddo. For all the kiddos, that lady said we lost on Naming Day. Now, every day they'll get a hug from me."

Sometimes, her sweetness could reduce me to a puddle. My mom gave me a baseball jersey, my dad gave me a magnifying glass, and Mesh gave me a Ken Griffey Jr. baseball card. It wasn't an original, but one of the residents reprinted various cards and sold them at the market.

"These gifts are cool!" I said, hugging them all in turn.

My dad loved his soap, and my mom got weepy when I brought out her flowers. They immediately took their place in the center of the table. Later that evening, our dinner was delivered, and we ate at our table. It was roasted chicken with stuffing, green beans with almonds, and berry pie for dessert. Even Libby had a feast of meat and chopped vegetables. When we were done, a bus came and gathered our dishes.

We didn't usually say grace, but on this day, we felt especially grateful. Our lives had been blessed with so many wonderful things, and we knew many people were not as fortunate. We made a commitment as a family that everyday we would give thanks for our blessings and pray for those less fortunate before we went to the diner.

After dinner, we took Libby for a walk along the lighted streets where people were singing long-ago songs called Christmas carols. December had been a month full of fun and excitement. How ironic, after a decade of wanting this existence, I needed downtime from too much happiness. The only feeling I should have is gratitude.

One of the first bills passed was to give adults one day off a month in addition to their two days a week. Though it was random which day one was granted, adults could request to share it with a spouse or friend. This month my parents got what was once a holiday called New Year's Day. It was like a birthday for the Earth. They let us stay home too.

The afternoon of January first found me sitting on the bleachers contemplating my new life and my ungracious feelings about it. Though my whole family had the day off, my parents must have felt the same because we didn't do anything special. We were also very low on credits, which limited our choices.

I wondered what the Daily I used to be would think of my spoiled brat melancholy state. It was then that I saw Officer Gray pull up in his cart.

"You look like your thoughts are about to leak out of your ears," he said as he climbed up and sat next to me.

"It's weird," I said, "but I was thinking about how crazy this month has been. I mean, it was all I wanted and better than I expected. It's been fun but busy, exciting but stressful. I feel drained. How can I think this way when I wished so hard for this kind of freedom?" I looked at him with a questioning smirk.

"Yeah," he grinned, "too much of anything is exhausting, whether it be good or bad. You need to find a way to chill out. How about I pick you up at your diner after dinner, around seven? If you get your parents' permission, I think I have just the thing."

"Yeah, see you at seven," he began to climb into his cart when I yelled, "What did she say?"

"Yes," he shouted with a smile and drove off.

After dinner, I sent Libby home with my family and waited for Gray. I was early, and I resumed my reflection of conflicting thoughts. Officer Gray pulled up and motioned for me to climb in. We turned down the west end corridor. He parked by the Defender storage door and walked across to the round sky room where we first entered New Haven. The room had since been named the Harold Seger Observatory. Gray went over to a panel, unlocked it, and operated the controls.

A vibrating hum began, and the dome above started rolling open. Little by little, the night sky came into view until the whole ceiling was filled with shining stars against the dark blackness of space. It was incredible. We rarely spent time outside at night as Dailys because of the curfew. But I had missed the sky, and maybe it's what I needed.

"How is there no snow weighing down on this dome?" I asked.

"While you only see the dome roll open, it is hidden under a spire-shaped structure camouflaged as part of the mountain. It is so steep that it sheds the snow, and the top opens like a flower. Though it is equipped with heated hinges, we are required to open and close it daily to keep it from freezing up. It's my favorite job," he smiled.

He grabbed two fold-out lounge chairs, and we opened them up to gaze upward effortlessly. Without taking his eyes off the inspirational view, he spoke with a tone of reverence. "My dad used to say, 'A man need only gaze at the night sky to reset his compass and realize he is but a speck in the great plan.' It is how I put my life in perspective."

"It does seem to free one from the burden of overthinking," I said with the same tone of awe in my voice.

We sat there for a good half hour not saying a word. Some people make silence uncomfortable, but we were content to quietly bathe in the vast providence of space.

CHAPTER 10

My friends and I went to the opening night of our baseball movie. I remembered how much I liked watching shows at the Hold, but the cushioned chairs, better screen, and crisp sound system intensified the experience. I was glad to hear we had thousands of files available.

We loved the movie, *The Rookie.* It was about a high school coach who, due to an injury, had given up his dream of being a professional baseball player. When his players saw him pitch, they talked him into trying out again. It was based on a true story. It showed that having dreams is never wrong, and it's worth fighting to make them happen.

We had to stifle our laughs when the video of my speech about the baseball club was shown. I was glad that Mrs. Riddley and Indy were taking charge of it. They found six more knowledgeable and willing adults to fill the coaching and umpire jobs. I just wanted to play, so I was relieved. So many people had signed up that we had three teams from each school and four adult teams.

With the baseball club safely in the hands of the recreation director and team organizers, my thoughts returned to the mysteries that were lying in wait for me. In my absence, my list of curiosities had grown, and its siren song had become impossible to ignore.

I was warned by the leaders to let the experts deal with these issues, but I was an expert too. They saw me as a child, an off-limits resource, but I am a Highmind specifically trained to decipher these mysteries. Solving the hidden and coded secrets was the key to addressing the threat looming over New Haven. It was equally likely that unraveling these secrets was required to free the outsiders from their tyrannical rulers. I knew I could help retrieve it, but I was going to have to prove it. Solving the hidden and coded secrets was the key to addressing the threat looming over New Haven. It was equally likely that unraveling these secrets was required to free the outsiders from their tyrannical rulers. I knew I could help retrieve it, but I was going to have to prove it.

I had exposed many of the castle's secrets, but knowing GD, I still had a long trail of clues to follow. The small scroll attached to the final step, which they took, was one thing that came to mind. Add to that the notes in GD's sketchbook, the strange marks on Vadina, and the intriguing nooks and crannies of GD's famous desk. And though Alec T. had been explained to me, I knew their explanation was sorely lacking in detail. And because they proved we were still in danger, I included Zoey's story, the repeated attacks on Ari and Jillian, and the one on me.

I started tri-column notes on each of these topics, but I decided GD's desk was the most accessible and logical place to start my search. The Defenders had this desk in storage for some time, and it was likely they searched it, but that was before they knew about the castle. They probably had no clue regarding GD's obsession with riddles and puzzles. And even if they did, no one knew GD's puzzles like me.

I lay under the desk with the flashlight Officer Gray gave me. I already knew of one hidden compartment, but it had been an easy find. It had contained my grandmother's jewelry for rainy-day bartering, but no contraband. My mom was overjoyed when I gave the pieces to her. But this desk had more secrets, of that, I was sure.

Libby cocked her head and brought me her ball as if she thought I was searching for it. I sat up and tossed it rebounding it off the hall wall and down the stairs. My mom hated it when I did that because it sent Libby scampering at full speed inside the house. I heard her irritated response as well as the laughter from Mesh and my dad. I laughed, knowing she found it amusing too, but she felt it was her job to be the voice of order.

Returning to my quest, I narrowed my focus on anything that could be a latch or unused space suggesting a secret compartment. On the side of the drawer, way toward the back, was a piece of wood that had no purpose. I could pull it a bit, but nothing happened.

I tried to pull the drawer out, but it was not designed to be detached from the desk. The area was too small to get my magnifying glass in there, so I felt around searching for anything that would hint at how such a mechanism would function. But I found nothing. I lay there studying my odd view when Mesh came in.

"What are you doing, Connor?" asked Meshka, holding Libby's ball.

"Oh," I startled. "I was using my new flashlight and playing detective."

"Can I play?" she asked with innocent gullibility.

"Sure," I said, and I scooted over, so she could fit next to me.

She was having fun shining the light into the darker recesses of the furniture to see what resided there. She held the tool at every angle, casting strange shadows. I was suddenly drawn to an irregular pattern revealed by her shadow play on the underbelly of the center drawer. When she tired of the game, she gave the flashlight back to me.

"Mom told me to tell you we're heading to dinner in twenty minutes," she said and trotted out my door.

I reached up and felt the subtle texture, confirming there was something painted on the surface. It was an invisible pigment and probably needed a certain light or chemical to bring it out. GD mentioned three types of reagents used to reveal invisible pigments. The problem was which one to try. They each had the potential to destroy the evidence if the wrong one was used. I needed to gather some things without arousing suspicion, so I could test the paint. I filled in my notes and stashed them in the compartment behind the left top drawer.

January was busy and speeding by, and with everything on my plate, I had little time to spend on the desk. The newly formed teams were trained enough to play, and games were starting in a week. With only one field, the schedule was tight. Practices would be held right after school for the younger teams not playing, and Sunday afternoons were open for the adults. Each team would play two games a week. The adult games would be played on Saturdays, and the middle school and high school teams would play Monday through Thursday evenings. The crowds were expected to dwindle from the first game because of the numerous competitions to choose from.

In my room. I thought back to that night sky. It was calming unless one considered its infinite power to devastate all the specks here on the Earth. However, it was true that much would change whether we survived or we didn't. The strangely comforting part was it was out of my hands. But figuring out this desk *was* in my hands, and I was determined to settle it.

I relocated the piece of wood that seemed to have no purpose. In frustration, I yanked on the small block with all my might and pulled it out completely. I was shocked and worried I had broken it until I saw the arrow it revealed. I flashed my light on the opposite side of the drawer and found a slot. I inserted the block into it, and I heard a clunk. Behind the drawer attached to the desktop, a thin scroll rolled out. It had strange squiggles splashed across the page in no particular pattern. It made no sense to the untrained eye, but I knew those lines. They were similar to the ones on the Vadina statue and the two on the sword scroll.

I copied them down on a separate piece of paper and noted them on my tri-column notes along with a notation to ask to see the Vadina statue. Though I have an eidetic memory, I still take notes so I can view all the pieces together outside of my head. Plus, I needed to get a better look at them with my magnifying glass. Hearing my mom and sister, I put everything away and went downstairs.

It was time to reexamine the markings on Vadina's base, so I began devising a way to be allowed to see them. Initially, I believed it was just a design. After all, it wasn't created by GD, so how could he leave clues on it? But it may prove A.L.E.C.T. is bigger than I originally thought. Tomorrow was Friday, and I didn't have practice or tutoring, so after school, I headed to the museum.

"Good afternoon, Connor. Have you come to check on your dragon before we put her in storage?"

It stunned me, but it shouldn't have. Every collection was on rotation to keep the exhibits fresh and interesting. Mr. Alex explained that each art selection was grouped by topic, date, and genre, allowing pieces to cross over into various groupings.

It had been more than three months since the museum had fully opened, so the few collections on display back then were overdue for rotation. Vadina had been part of the first two displays. I had neglected my investigations, and now I may lose the chance to inspect it. He had called it my dragon. If only it were mine.

"Yes," I answered, "I was wondering if I could look at the whole piece, including the base. There was a cool design on it I think, but I've forgotten," I said, hoping he was unaware of my abilities.

"Well, I could use some extra help packing up these displays and bringing out the new ones. We were going to start tonight after closing at 7:00, but we can start moving some things early. If you stay for a few hours, you can earn some credits."

"Done, but can we start with Vadina now, so I can take a little time to see her one last time?"

He lifted the statue out of its glass case with such care that I felt bad about how casually I had handled it so many months ago. He rolled up a cart, settled her softly on a velvet-covered plate, and adjusted the stabilizers at each corner. I followed him into the workroom, where he moved the statue and plate onto a table.

"I know you think the world of this piece, but I am asking you not to touch it. You can spin the inspection platform to see every side." Then he showed me how to use the magnifying lens with the overhead light.

"This is super cool," I said.

"Okay, I have some work to get to, so I'll leave you to your task. There is a camera and intercom, so if you have any trouble or questions, just talk out loud and I will hear you."

I wasn't sure if that was a kind gesture or a warning, but it didn't matter. I had no intention of doing anything unsanctioned to this treasure.

"Thank you, Mr. Walker. Don't worry, I won't let anything happen to her."

I used the overhead light and slowly inspected every inch of the statue. I carefully recorded the markings and noted the placement and order of each one. I thought I saw tiny flaws on the ends of several of the lines, and I wanted a closer look.

I took my magnifying glass out of my pocket and added its strength to the overhead. *Bingo! I was right.* There were tiny deviations on the ends of six of the marks. What could they mean? I recorded each one then I carefully looked again to be sure I hadn't missed any.

It wasn't long after that Mr. Walker called for my help. I yelled I was coming, but I paused and said goodbye to *my* dragon, and I wondered when I would see her again.

I wasn't allowed to handle the artwork. My job was to break down and move the display cases, pull the description cards from their slots, and file them. Mr. Walker said his schedule was not on its original timetable because, like many municipal buildings, its opening was fraught with delays and mishaps. He said that when he got back on schedule, he would rotate in a couple of new exhibits every month. Though some pieces would return, they would be grouped differently, giving the museum goers a variety of perspectives.

I enjoyed learning about museum protocol from Fin and Brooke, Mr. Walker's assistants, while we ate a delivered dinner together. There was more to it than I ever imagined. Seven-thirty snuck up on me, and I had to go home.

"Did you say goodbye to your dragon?" my dad asked.

"Yes, as well as the many other pieces I enjoyed. Mr. Walker assures me the next collection will be just as interesting. I can't wait to see it."

"Wow, I didn't know we had so many works of art to show," my mom expressed with her hand on her chest.

"Not all are art, per se. Some displays are about history, and others are science-related, but yeah, he has several shipping containers of stuff. There is a horseshoe-shaped barrier of containers at each end of the tunnel, and they have hundreds of tons of stuff for our town."

"Sounds like something we shouldn't know," my dad responded.

"Well, I don't know how we could get to it. It's crazy guarded. Mr. Walker had to fill out forms, and he and his assistants had to be escorted by Defenders to get what he needed. He said our laws and security protocols prevent officials and residents from exploiting it."

"Maybe we *should* know," my mom offered, "so we don't worry about running low on supplies." I suspected her job involved some knowledge of the town's inventory, but her reasonable conclusion had my dad nodding his head.

I took Libby for a short walk. Tonight, I would re-look at the curvy lines on the scroll tucked in GD's desk. I was interested to see if they had any tiny irregular marks on the ends like the ones on Vadina.

I waited until Mesh was in bed. My parents were cuddled on the couch, locked into a historical documentary. I stretched my shoulders, presented them a large yawn, and told them goodnight. Stopping at the restroom under the stairs, I readied myself for bed, went to my room, and closed my door.

Gathering my flashlight and magnifying glass, I crawled under my desk. It took only seconds to go through the puzzle moves that pulled the scroll down. The position was awkward, but I strained in various positions, painstakingly looking for the irregularities.

There they were, six notches, and they were the perfect inverses of the ones on Vadina.

CHAPTER 11

I was charged up about our next game. This week four teams would be eliminated. If we held our rank, we'd be in the championship game.

It was difficult to practice as a team because our only field was heavily used. We had one practice hour a week on the field. The rest of the time we were relegated to playing catch where we could, practicing with digital programs, or reserving one of the two batting cages at Wally's. It was fair because it was the same for all the teams, but after the next playoff games, we'll have two more practice sessions on the field.

I was on my way home to change for dinner when I saw Rand. He was the tech guru, Tage. GD had named him specifically on the castle scroll, and I wondered if he knew my grandad.

"Hi, Mr. Lewis sir."

"Oh please, and I do mean, please. Call me Rand," he responded.

"Or Tage," I quipped back.

"No, not that. It's classified," he warned.

"Sorry, don't worry. I haven't said anything about that meeting. Hayden was the only person who knew about the castle, and I haven't told him I got it back yet. It's hidden in my closet."

"You *are* good at keeping secrets," he smiled. "Most kids would burst if they couldn't say something."

"Well, I've had to keep secrets my whole life. No one knew I was a Highmind, or that GD taught me how to solve puzzles and mysteries." I paused for a minute.

"Something on your mind Connor?" he asked.

"Did you know my grandad?"

"I knew *of* your grandad, and he knew of me, but we never met."

"Oh," I said with defeat.

"Sorry, kid. Everyone made a point of not knowing who was involved."

"I understand that, but I'm not going to give up hope of finding someone who knew him."

"Well, I bet there are a few stories your parents haven't told you yet. You should ask them," he said and gave me a thumbs-up as he left. I wondered if enough time had passed that my mom wouldn't be sad if I brought him up. It was worth a try.

After a difficult calculus test, I had time to get back to the squiggly lines. The desk scroll and the base each contained six notched symbols. I did not see the sword symbols close enough to notice notches, but my guess was there was some kind of key to connect them. It was obvious they went together. It was easy to fit the ones with marks at the ends, but how they fit together and what they meant eluded me.

The desk scroll displayed the marks in a scattered pattern down the long scroll, and it occurred to me that perhaps the order wasn't random. I needed to remove the document, so I could work with it on a flat surface.

I crawled back under the desk and unfurled the document. Feeling around, I could tell it was on a spring-loaded rod. I shook it and it rocked back and forth in its slots. I was about to call it a night when I located a small lump on one end. Pushing it released the rod from its home.

I poured over the two sets of wavy lines and thought of various ways to connect them. I tried to plan what had to be done, but after an hour, my focus was waning. I secured my desk and went to bed to give it fresh eyes tomorrow.

Today was Thursday, and we were in the thick of the final playoff games. The last high school playoff game was tonight, and the last two adult playoffs were on Saturday. Our deciding game wasn't until Sunday, but early Saturday morning we had an hour to use the field. Practices were in the morning, then prepped for the two adult playoff games that afternoon and evening. It would be a busy Saturday, and I knew I would be too tired to examine the scroll and the Vadina marks. I may not be able to commit to the investigation until after baseball ends.

My friends and I returned after lunch to watch Hannah's team. A significant number of the players on the adult teams were Defenders. They were incredible athletes and fun to watch. Though their experience as ball players was lacking, they made up for it with sheer power and agility.

I discovered Officer Gray had an adopted brother, Axle, who was the captain of one of the adult teams. Axle had joined the Takota family as a child. They were fiercely loyal and close, but they could fight just as hard. It made me wish I had a brother. Even though I had my three close friends, we still had secrets, big ones. But with all the subtle gestures between these two men, it didn't look like they held much from each other. I wanted that.

It was just past six when Hannah's team was called the winner. I congratulated her and headed to my diner. My family knew I'd be late, and they had already finished. I told them to head home, and I'd follow up with Libby. I saw Ari and Jilly at another table, and they asked me to join them.

"How have you been, Connor? The only time we see you lately is at the games."

"I know. I feel like I am as busy now as I ever was, but I like what I'm doing, so I guess I'm lucky. How about you two? Your boyfriend ties up your time like baseball does mine."

"Well, I guess we're lucky too," Ari laughed. She turned to Jilly, her eyes sparkling with happiness.

"I learned Officer Gray has a brother," I said.

"Yes, Axle. Those two are thick as thieves, as my father would say," Jilly exclaimed.

"I've never heard you talk about your father," I stated. "What was he like?"

"Umm, he was a history teacher," she stuttered.

"He died several years ago. We miss him terribly," Ari jumped in. The sparkle in her eyes was replaced with concern.

The looks between them confirmed my suspicions. There was more to their story. I always questioned how they healed from their attack without demonstrating any tenderness or pain. They received serious gunshot wounds one day, but within a week they were perfectly healed. It didn't add up, but I had more than my share of inquiries right now.

They walked part of the way with me, but I was taking the long way home to walk Libby. I had been neglecting her since baseball started, and I needed time for introspection. I intended to evaluate all my projects to prioritize and schedule my time. I put baseball at the top of my list because we were so close to the championship. Tutoring, Libby, and my mounting investigations would rise back to the top after next weekend. I felt more settled as I walked. I tried to focus on what I needed to shore up to be on my best game, but the squiggly lines kept bubbling up in my brain.

We won our game on Sunday, solidifying our place in the final match. When I got home, my parents had planned a surprise night at the movie house to celebrate. I knew I wouldn't get to my project tonight, but I was excited to see the movie that had started showing yesterday, *Star* Wars: *The New Hope.*

The baseball movie was good, and I enjoyed it, but this movie was mind-blowing. I had to watch it again. The trailers afterward showed there were more chapters to this saga, and I couldn't wait to see them.

I suddenly thought of our tubular town differently. It was like a spaceship sheltering us from the harsh environment outside and protecting us from our enemies. Life in space was a completely new idea to me, but I was fascinated by the concept. I talked my friends into seeing it.

I still had tutoring on Tuesdays and Thursdays, so my team planned to practice on Wednesdays where we could until we got the field on Friday. It worked out well and allowed me to pick up Meshka after she attended her post-school activities.

But today was Monday, and I had several hours to myself. I went straight home to have time alone in my room. I took out the desk scroll and the ones I meticulously copied from Vadina's base. The ones on the scroll were in a scattered pattern, but the ones on Vadina were in a neat line across the bottom.

I copied the Vadina marks and numbered and cut them out. I started by matching the notched ones, but that gave me six separate pieces of unrecognizable symbols. Then I started with the first one on the left front side of the statue, but that wasn't right either. After thinking about it, I laid out the scroll and added the Vadina lines to the scroll pattern. I continue to place them using their original order, easily joining the lines one after the other. Could it be this simple?

When I finished, I had a weird drawing that looked like a fractured river or a vascular system with fingering off-shoots that just ended. I had never seen anything like it. It was either correct, which was baffling, or I was on the wrong track completely. Regardless, it was turning out to be a difficult puzzle.

It was a bit of a letdown because I had no idea where to go from here. There were no letters or numbers to guide me. I could think of no lesson I had learned that came close to these strange lines.

I got on my tablet, but without a word to describe it, my search was fruitless. I put everything back in its hidden places and closed my tablet. Maybe if I let it bounce around in my head, something would stand out, or make some kind of sense.

"Come on, Libby, it's time to pick up Meshka, and I feel like a treat." Homemade ice cream was available at the diner today, and it would be fun to surprise her.

The championship games were the talk of the town. It had been an amazing season. I never imagined baseball would catch on so quickly. I guess people had been craving competitive excitement without knowing it. The combined band from both schools had been practicing the United States anthem and would perform it at all three games. It made me regret not suggesting we come up with names for our teams, but for the first year, it was decided the level and letter would suffice. Our level was 1, the high school was 2, and the adults were 3. My team was 1C, and we were playing 1A.

I took a walk with Libby the evening before the game. It was late, and the sun lights were omitting a purple and pink hue against the northern walls, slowly merging with the blue cloudlike pattern. Within the hour, the gentle glow would turn into a dark, speckled ceiling to simulate a starlit sky.

The engineers had done everything to ensure the inhabitants would not miss the feeling of being outside. The irony was that most Dailys had spent their lives cocooned within the walls of their workplace or their homes for safety. Some people had outside jobs, but it was unlikely they paid much attention to the skies unless they were threatening.

Haru said these additions were necessary to promote joy, comfort, and trust in the life that *could* be. The goal of New Haven, we were often told, was to acclimate us to liberty. Once people understand and experience freedom, they don't forget it, and they fight to keep it. The irony was we had to learn this lesson while isolated and detained within the tunnels.

I came to the park and saw Hannah sitting on the bleachers. Although I added an official title to every other Defender's name, I didn't call her Defender or Officer Hannah; she was just Hannah. I saw her often when

I visited the rec room, and every time she scolded me for not calling it Wally's. It became an ongoing joke.

I climbed up on the bleachers and sat next to her. We were silent and staring out at the vacant field. Fridays were reserved for any activity but baseball. Most of the week we took it over, and even though it was sparsely used on its off time, it was only right that it be available.

"How are you doing? Does the game have you wound up?" she asked me without taking her eyes off the field.

"Yes, the jitters are fierce today. I should have brought a ball to throw for Libby, but I felt I should relinquish the field to the non-baseballers," I said while watching a family that had just arrived. I felt Libby was straining a bit, wanting to join in their game of Frisbee. "Stay girl," I commanded softly, and she sat back down intently watching the activity. "I wish my mind behaved like Libby."

"Yeah, it's hard to control the barking in your head when you're the dog and the master," she laughed. She had a wonderful laugh. It was rich and gentle at the same time.

"I have only recently learned the game of baseball, but I know about battles. Sports are a kind of battle, and though the players aren't risking life or limb, the loss is real."

"What do you do to prepare for battle?" I asked sincerely.

"The key is not to focus on the whole event or the result. The key is to be present in the moments of engagement. In other words, quit thinking about the score, just play ball, and play hard." We both watched the family laugh and play, enjoying the pure simplicity of fun.

"Maybe another key is to tap into the joy of the game. It's a privilege to play it, and it makes me want to do well."

"Now you've got it," and she smiled at me. We talked about many more things on those bleachers while various visitors strolled past the park. She made it easy to glide from one topic to the next, laughing and meshing between each seamlessly.

I slept well that night and woke up ready for the big day. Our game was first, and then the high school game would start. The adult game was tomorrow.

Ten O'clock in the morning was game time, and at nine, I tugged on my red t-shirt with 1C and Home written in white letters on the front. Each player had been issued one reversible baseball jersey that worked for both home and visitor games. I looked at myself in the mirror, remembering when Mr. Vogel presented them to us.

The game opened with the band playing the anthem, while a girl from High school sang the words. She had an amazing voice. When the song ended, the game started with the first pitch thrown out by the top player from the eliminated team.

Though big hits, fast pitches, and impressive plays made the first three innings exciting, the game held tight without a run on the board. During the fourth inning, the other team was leading by two runs due to errors.

We scored three outs before more damage was done. It was the bottom of the last inning, and I could see the pressure eating away at my team's resolve. I needed to do something before we got up to bat. I recalled the conversation I had with Hannah.

"Remember when we first started playing? It was so much fun to just play the game. No matter how this plays out, this is the last inning of the season. Let's play like we used to. Let's play hard and have fun. Don't look at the scoreboard, just play ball." The spectators and even the other team looked over as shouts and high-fives rallied through our dugout.

"Okay," I ended with, "just hit the ball-HTB. We got this!" they all responded with a resounding "HTB, HTB," as our first batter, Mary, headed to the plate.

The pitcher seemed slightly rattled by our display of solidarity and threw three balls in a row. The next was a reset, with a whiz past the plate. The count was three and one. The pitcher had to throw a strike, but Mary was ready for it. *SWACK!* She delivered a lead-off double.

Next was Kato. Though he was thrown out at first, Mary advanced to third with a laser focus on our first score. Jade got a walk to first. We had two on the base corners and one out. Hope was soaring, and our excitement was contagious as the crowd participation increased. The next batter got a double, sending Mary home and leaving players poised on second and third. We had one out, two on base, and the score was their team two and us one. Hayden walked out to the mound, and the pitcher did not argue when he took his place.

He made quick work of the next batter with a foul and two strikes. Two outs, but we had two scores just hanging out there waiting for their chance to stomp that home plate. If we tied it up, we'd get another chance with a sixth inning. I gripped the bat, walked out, and swung it assertively before I settled in the box.

Hayden knows me and my style better than anyone, and he's been playing longer than everyone. Everyone except me. I taught him, and I had a bead on his style too. It felt right that no matter what happened, it all came down to this moment. I stared him down. He smiled a no-mercy glare right back at me. It was why we were here— for the challenge, to push ourselves into those uncharted waters, for fun.

"Ball," the ump called.

"Foul," was the next call. Next pitch, "foul." I hit four more fouls in a row. It was time, and I dug in. I was going to clobber that ball and rip its cover to pieces with everything I had inside of me.

It came down the pike and curved just a little, just right. The solid *whack* was followed by a crazy crowd jumping up and down as it hit the home run section of the wall. I was so into the moment; it took a second to realize we had won. The final score was us four, them two.

Hayden and I shook hands and broke out a hug and a back slap. "Nicely done, Condor Man," he said. "I thought I had you, but nicely done."

"You didn't make it easy, Hays. I guess you had a good teacher," I said with a teasing raised eyebrow.

"Yeah, Coach Gray has been amazing," we both laughed. But it was true; he was an amazing coach. GD would have been a great coach too. He would have loved being a part of this. I thought of the friendships he would have made, friendships I have included him in by sharing memories of him. Yeah, I still miss him.

CHAPTER 12

My friends and I returned to the field after lunch to see the high school game. It amazed me how much further and faster the high school players could throw a ball. Noah's team claimed the season title.

The next day we watched the adult game at Kato's house. The dining hall gave us popcorn because they said we brought baseball and joy to the town. I don't think we can claim all that, but we took the popcorn with a thank you and a smile. The adult game was a powerhouse of young men and women in the prime of their lives and with their abilities. Axle's team won by one.

The season was over, and the residents asked what sport would be next. Basketball and volleyball were being discussed because they had been introduced at the Hold. Convenience ended up making the final decision. Two volleyball courts with bleachers and a concession stand fit nicely in the park and would be easy to set up. A basketball court would take more time, so volleyball was scheduled to start in April.

Another new activity was introduced that intrigued me, swimming. It seemed like the perfect pastime. It didn't require a commitment, and it might be just what I needed to unwind and refocus.

It was in a large building next to the gym called the Season Room. It featured a man-made pond called a swimming pool. It could hold a lot of water at thirty feet long and twenty-three feet wide. Though the Season Room opened a month ago, I hadn't seen it yet.

Hayden, Kato, Teke, and I hadn't gone yet, and the first visit was free. We weren't sure what to expect. None of us had ever gone swimming on the outside. Why would we? People drown in water. Walking into the lobby, we could hear the sound of shuffling feet and voices echoing above. We approached the counter, and a woman Defender greeted us. The ceiling slanted down behind her, and I concluded the pool with its many thousands of gallons of water, weighed heavily on the other side of it.

Shelves of puffy vests and polystyrene rings were lined up behind her. We chose the floatation rings with shoulder straps and a belt that cinched around our waist. She gave us a monotone run-down of the rules as if she had said it too many times, handed us each a towel, and pointed to the changing and bathroom area.

When we were issued shorts with built-in netted underwear at the Hold, I thought it was for when wash day had gotten behind, but it was for swimming. We changed into them and attached our floatation rings around us. I felt ridiculous as I bumbled my way up the stairs to the pool.

The lobby wasn't particularly dark, but the pool room was noticeably brighter. Benches were draped with towels, and sandals littered the ground. A narrow L-shaped catwalk ran down one edge and across the end where a Defender in swimming trunks sat on a lifeguard chair. Children splashed in the shallow end, and we awkwardly maneuvered our girthy-ringed bodies past them and into the water. It was chilly but refreshing.

When we reached the point where our feet left the bottom, we experienced the sensation of floating. It was slightly distressing, but with our arms over the rings, our upper bodies were well above the water. Officer Gray's brother, Axle, swam by us without floatation help. He glided through and underneath the water like he was born to it.

"How are you staying afloat?" I asked.

"I'm swimming. It's an amazing feeling. It's like being weightless, and the cool water makes my body feel like my blood is minty," he smiled, showing his revelry.

"Minty blood?" I questioned.

"Remember the first time you brushed your teeth with minty toothpaste," he explained, "and then you pulled air across your teeth? It was refreshing and invigorating, right?"

We all remembered and nodded in response.

"That's how swimming makes your whole body feel. If you want to learn, I can teach you. If I teach a class of three or more students, we all get in for free for the lesson times. I get pool time, and you guys can learn to swim without those dorky rings. What do you say?"

"Absolutely," we said together, but I was suddenly fixated on the fact I was wearing something dorky. Many others were using the floatation equipment, but he was right. It made us look like we didn't belong in the water.

"Okay, I'll sign you up to take lessons from me. How about we meet every Wednesday at 4:00?"

"Yeah, cool, thanks," we spoke, overlapping our responses. I was taking up a new sport after all.

Our March autumn was evident as the green-leaved branches slowly began to be replaced with fall-colored ones. Our seasons naturally moved gently from one to the next in a familiar order. And though our dates were off, we learned the seasons and months in the southern hemisphere were also reversed.

Jilly and Ari's neighbor, Billie, had her baby in February, but I had been too busy to visit. She only lived one house down from me, but I justified my poor social graces by telling myself she was busy too. It was the weekend, and I had nothing pressing. It was time I met my new neighbor.

I knocked and Officer Gabe, her husband, opened the door.

"Connor, come in. Did you come to see me or the baby?"

"Well, it's always nice to see you, Officer Gabe …" he put his hand up to stop me.

"Look, I know we're supposed to encourage kids to respect our titles, but it gives me a weird vibe when you say Officer. We're neighbors, so unless you're here on official business," he chuckled, "just call me Gabe."

I laughed. "Okay, Gabe," I said, drawing out his name, "I was wondering if I could see baby Katie."

"Sure, Hannah is upstairs with Billie and the baby, but we'll be leaving soon. Hannah hadn't seen her yet, so we made a quick stop."

I trotted up the stairs and saw the woman in the small bedroom painted a delicate pink with gentle puffy clouds decorating the walls. Hannah was sitting in a rocking chair, holding the sleeping child in her arms. She had that wistful look in her eyes that said she might like a child of her own someday.

They both gave me the quiet sign, and I silently walked over to Hannah and Katie. She was a beautiful baby with wispy brown curls and a pouty little mouth. She began to stir as if she knew something in her small world had changed.

Hannah whispered, "You said she's gained over a pound already. I'll need to keep up with my visits, or I won't even recognize her. Thanks for letting me hold her, but it's time to get back to work." She tried to gently hand her back to Billie, but little Katie opened her eyes, and I could see her winding up to make noise.

"Connor, could you take her for just a minute? I need to tell Gabe something before they leave."

She didn't wait for me to agree; she just stuck the now full-on crying infant in my arms. I remember walking around with one of the babies at Rita's, the woman who watched me after my mom died. I positioned Katie so my right forearm supported her belly and her head nestled in the crook of my left elbow. Her tiny limbs hung lazily over both sides of my arms, and I bounced her gently as I strolled back and forth in the small room.

She quieted down immediately, and I felt her relax and fall back to sleep. I continued my walk, noticing the little decorations and tiny clothing on the changing table. A small wooden carving of a pony standing on the windowsill caught my eye. It was well done, and leaning down, I saw Gray's name on it. Seven shiny stars dangled from a spinning moon mobile. They danced on their strings over her bed with the slow spin of the swirling globe. The blanket I saw my mother working on was draped over the side of the crib. For only being alive a month, the kid's room had as much stuff in it as mine.

Billie came back in ready to take the newborn, but she stopped when she saw us.

"Connor, where did you learn to hold a baby like that?"

"I'm sorry, Billie. Rita, a lady who watched me, taught me to do this with crying babies. I wouldn't have dropped her."

"Wow, Connor, she's so comfortable. I fed her about thirty minutes ago, and she always goes to sleep and then wakes up and cries for a bit. But look at you go. She looks so relaxed."

I smiled. "Sounds like she gets a bad tummy after eating. Rita said it puts pressure on the tummy where the bubbles build up."

"Oh, my gosh. You'd make an amazing babysitter," she said with a smile and a tilt of her head.

"Uh, well," I stammered, "I don't know. She is so little. But I could watch her if my mom was around."

"That would be amazing. We have friends who say they'll watch her, but that means we can't go out with them. We can pay you in credits," she added.

"No, I think this is just stuff neighbors do for each other. I earn enough credits. I'm good."

After dinner, I settled into my room. I told my mom about maybe watching Katie with me, and she was thrilled. How do I keep adding tasks to my list? I already have too many.

I went up to my room to work on my calculus homework. Both my parents were stunned that I was learning such high-level studies. Nothing I worked on was at my grade level. In the Hold, I was in the fifth grade, and four months ago I moved to sixth. As of last week, I am a seventh grader at the high school, but all my studies are at the college level.

They wanted to slow my social advancement and maintain my interactions with kids my age. Social development occurs in phases of brain growth, and it can't be acquired through books alone. It requires extensive experimentation with one's peers. Most of the time I liked the situation, but it was also frustrating.

As a Daily, I hid my intelligence, so I wouldn't be sent to the Highmind camp, but I had GD to talk to. Now I hide it so I don't intimidate people, and I have no one to talk to. Everyone in my class was appropriately placed academically, but me. I felt like my dog, being held back by loyalty and a leash. And like her, I respected those boundaries, but also like her, I wanted to run with someone who could keep up with me.

I was always given privacy to work on my homework, which also provided me lots of mystery time. Closing my completed homework page, I pulled out the combined lines and studied the strange pattern it created. It must be a river that travels across a rugged terrain. I wondered where the lines from the sword scroll would fit. I put it away and took out GD's sketchbook. Maybe his notes could point me to an answer.

He had made notations and drawings on many of the pages, so it was going to take a while to sort them out. At first glance, one might think GD was a doodler, but he wasn't. He was a man on a quest who needed to get his message to those who could carry the plan forward.

Some entries were beyond my scope at this time, but the highlighted words on the first nine pages intrigued me. Nine words, one on each page, were underlined with a yellow pencil. They were key art concepts, and it would be logical to highlight them for easy reference. But I was certain GD left clues in this book for me. I wrote those words down in order: nature, distinctive, intensity, saturation, contrast, garish, vibrance, unvalued, and middle.

The first eight words were related to art, but the last one seemed random, so I knew it was part of a code. I played with the first and last letters of each word, and then it occurred to me. Maybe the order had something to do with which letters were significant. I tried a simple pattern using the first word, first letter; second word, second letter, and so on. That brought me to N I T U R H T G, but the last word did not contain enough letters to complete the pattern.

NITUR wasn't a word, but NITU was. It was a Hindu word, often used as a female name meaning moral, beautiful, or eternal. Interesting because this quest was all about ethical goals, but it gave me no direction. It did make me believe Nitu was the first word.

Maybe I had to start the pattern over with the last five words. That gave me a word I had heard before, CABAL.

A cabal is a secret group scheming to overthrow a government. So, a beautiful, eternal, and moral rebellion, that sounded very GD. Though I knew it was the intended answer, it revealed no illuminating secrets. There was another step to this riddle, but it was time to get some sleep, and I fell quickly into a dream.

I looked through the hazy darkness of my old room. I was very young. My grandad had just finished telling me a story. Then he stood up and whispered. "Nitu Cabal. It is your destiny, Connor. You must find it. You are the only one who can. Find Cali ..."

I awoke with a start. It wasn't just a dream; it was a memory. GD was standing over my toddler bed. I stared up at him as he was whispering to find Cali. I was shrouded in a fog of doubt that it was a true memory. Doubt, because I was only an infant. Doubt, because I had never heard of anyone with the name Cali. But he said *it*, not who. What could *it* be? A thing, a place, a concept? I retrieved my hidden notes and wrote *Cali* down. It took some time before I could fall back to sleep.

The town began emergency drills for three different lockdown scenarios. One was called the Disaster Drill and required evacuation to a safe part of the tunnel. The second was the Quarantine Drill, which involved containment, and the last was the Hostile Force Drill, which addressed violent acts being committed near and/or in the tunnel. It was smart because all these things could happen, and they each required a different response. But I couldn't help but wonder if it was about new intel.

The first drills involved fire, and each tunnel section was given an evacuation site to get to. It did not go well because the residents took too much time trying to save and haul their belongings. It was retaught before we moved on to the Quarantine Drill. That went smoother since people were simply instructed to stay in place.

But the one that caused the most anxiety was the Hostile Force Drill. I immediately thought of Zoey and her situation. I wondered if it upset her, but I saw her that day after school, and she seemed unaffected. They said it addressed crime, and many called it the crime drill, but it was also geared to prepare us for an invasion. I assumed, and hoped, in that case, trained adults would gather weapons and set up strategic defenses.

March quickly passed without much progress on the coded sketchbook, and April was winking at May. I would say it was a nice day, but because every day had mild weather, days were no longer distinguished by that. It was its events. And though it was an ordinary day, my friends and I were feeling particularly happy. It had been weeks since we had checked out the baseball equipment, but we decided to play our three-on-one game. At Wally's, Hannah met us at the counter, like always.

"Hey, how are my Hall of Famers doing?"

"Well, that's a stretch," I laughed.

"Yeah, but we'll take it," quipped Hayden.

"We're here for baseball equipment. We're going to play some catch today. It's been a while and we miss it," Teke stated.

"I wish I could go and throw a couple with you," she said with a melancholy tone.

"Is something up? I mean, you could get someone to cover and throw a few with us. You've done it before," Kato suggested.

I had a bad vibe from her, so I asked. "Is something wrong? Are you having someone else take over this job?"

"Oh, no. I wouldn't give up this gig," she answered quickly and confidently. "It's my favorite part of being a Defender."

"Well," Teke said, "you know you can join us any time you want. How about this Friday at 3:30?" We all nodded with our approval.

"You got it. It's a date," she said with renewed enthusiasm radiating in her smile.

It's odd how a simple interaction suddenly reveals a significant and obvious truth when looking back on it. The oddness of it doesn't resonate enough to make one stop and take note. But later, it evolves into a defining moment.

On Wednesday, Axle canceled our last swimming lesson. But even that didn't alert us to the news coming our way. On Thursday, we discovered Hannah died on an offsite mission.

We were told via our tablet feed that seven Defenders had died and several more were injured, one critically. They were meeting at the Hold to pull in the Defenders from the off-site bunkers, and a Dranger team ambushed them. The report stated that no enemies escaped with information regarding the Hold or New Haven. But I was suspicious. It was the third attack on the Hold that I knew of.

I read her obituary as well as those of the other six soldiers. She grew up a Daily, like me, and she and Axle had been best friends since childhood. It filled in her connection to this project. Gray, no doubt, took her on to be part of New Haven. I bet Axle was devastated, and I also bet Officer Gray blamed himself.

I mourned my loss and for all who knew her. She was a good person. I knew this heavy darkness would last for a long time. Grief creates a bleak web that spiders out into every corner of one's mind. It sets up a permanent home in every related memory, and when plucked, it binds itself to more.

As if the article writer knew he needed to relieve his readers' suffering, he interjected some lighter news. We were getting several new Defenders from the off-sites, and we should welcome them into our community. There would be a video feed introducing them after they spent quarantine time in the surveillance sites at the edge of the barrier.

In the last paragraph, information was given regarding a memorial wall being erected in the corridor in front of the church. It would hold the names of all the Defenders who died in service. It would also hold the names of residents, including people involved with the tunnel but didn't make it. As far as I knew, only one resident had died, but it was a secret. I wondered how that would be handled. The report ended with a message thanking, honoring, and promising to remember them.

CHAPTER 13

The single memorial service turned into three due to the number of people who wanted to attend. Two would be held at the church and one in Treagan Park, which would also be on a video feed. Dailys were familiar with death, but getting together due to it was a new concept for us. And attending church after a decade of religion being illegal was still uncomfortable for some.

When a Daily died, the family had to report the death within hours and grieve before the body was hauled off for public safety reasons. Friends and loved ones gave their messages of sympathy in passing encounters because Dailys weren't allowed to have gatherings of any kind. Although we had experienced several community events since we left that life, assembling over a tragedy left us unsure of the etiquette it entailed.

Only Defenders were allowed at the first service since none of the fallen soldiers had any family members. My family received invitations to the second service, which centered on Hannah. Although we grieved deeply for the other six Defenders, this was Hannah's hometown, and many people knew her.

We walked by the New Haven Memorial Wall project that was in progress. The frames encased the empty black spaces matching my mood. It was little consolation that they would eventually fill with names. Inside the church, colorful glass scenes in the upper area of the room lit up the acts of kindness depicted in them. We sat down on the richly stained pews facing the podium, where the relief of a man stood with outstretched arms beckoning his flock to come to him.

Haru opened the service with a prayer and spoke the seven Defenders' names. The six offsite soldiers' names caused us to reflect on the tragedy, but when he read Hannah's name, it felt like getting punched in the gut. Humans think with words, and I think names are the most powerful. I wondered if parents thought about that when they chose them.

Then he read a couple of verses from his religious books and asked for a moment of silence to remember our fallen soldiers. I felt tears rolling down my face, and though I was unsure if it was allowed, I didn't care. I remembered Hannah's kind smile and warm laugh greeting us on our frequent visits to Wally's, the smile and laugh that she took with her. I thought of the first time I met her in the Hold infirmary after I had been abducted. I was so afraid, but she made me feel safe and calmed my fears. Gulping back the sobs that threatened to break free, I noticed Mesh watching me with such concern that I reached over and grabbed her hand.

"I'm okay," I whispered. But I wasn't. The dark vines of loneliness crept through my mind, reminding me how isolated I was. I needed Hannah to talk with, laugh with, and encourage me to fight through the fears that held me back. I needed GD to guide me through his secrets to save this dream that people I love keep dying to preserve. Once more I found myself alone on that island surrounded by new moon darkness and unknown foes.

Gabe spoke of the soldiers' service, and others spoke of what they were like off duty. Officer Gray came and played guitar while a woman sang a sad goodbye song. Haru spoke of the importance of going through grief and how it honored what was sacrificed. Sad as it was, I think the gathering was beneficial. It lasted just under an hour, and as difficult as the emotions it evoked were, I had the chance to honor my friend, thank her, tell her I loved her, and say goodbye.

My sorrow wasn't gone, but my friend and her fellow soldiers had a dignified finale. It was cathartic to hear stories about her and know she would live on in the memories of so many. When we lost my grandad, we weren't allowed to have a service, and I remember how alone I felt. Although it still feels awful, it feels better than sitting on my porch desperately trying to wish GD back.

Why hadn't I prepared myself to lose people after settling in this town? It was an ignorant viewpoint because Ari, Jilly, and I were attacked at the Hold. Zoey was kidnapped and held hostage by her aunt for at least a month, and who knows what else has occurred, all while under Defender protection. Why had I let down my guard?

I remember following my parents from place to place without knowing where they were leading us. I knew my dad couldn't magically protect us, but there was nowhere else I wanted to be, so I bore the consequences of staying together. I had many reservations regarding the Hold, but safety wasn't one of them until I was kidnapped.

When we arrived at this town, once again, I believed with a naïve innocence that the world couldn't break through the massive barrier of the mountain. But the immorality of the world was in here too. Even our leaders, though they were good-hearted, had things to answer for.

The Defenders stood bravely as part of our protective barrier guarding us and our tunnel home. But I hadn't walked that thought through until now. They sacrificed all they had to save us. It was comforting and chilling at the same moment. It was true that our streets were safe from even the smallest of crimes, but that brought Zoey's aunt to mind. Life always throws in a caveat.

It took days to rally through my deliberations, but it did settle two things. One, it reinforced the need to resolve these mysteries before anyone else died. Eventually, the Corporates would find us, and we could not win the battle they would bring. Two, it helped me sort out my grief and share it, which I did. I thought it could set Zoey on a healing path too. But I had to be careful how I approached it.

It had been over a week since the big loss, and I went next door to babysit Katie while Billie and Gabe had a meal by themselves. Gabe opened the door with a bruised cheek and the remnants of a split lip.

"Wow, Gabe," I said. "You need to watch out for those doors. They're a formidable foe."

"Ha ha," he answered.

"I'd ask what happened, but you probably aren't going to tell me," I said.

"No, I can tell you. Gray, Axle, and I had a boxing go at the gym." He stated, but I didn't get why they wanted to pummel each other.

If May was the mid-point of spring, it was the tunnel's mid-point of fall, and the leaves about town were rich with warm hues. I hadn't gone to Wally's to check out equipment since Hannah died. I couldn't face going there and not seeing her. I justified it by saying I was focusing on my other responsibilities and trying new activities, like swimming.

Much excitement was circulating about June's new diversion coming to the Season Room and the public opening of the observatory. Everyone was talking about the pool in the Season Room being transformed into a beach scene with palm trees, sand-like flooring, and a wave pool. Several sky and environmental programs would enhance the experience.

They planned varying evening programs as well as sunsets, star-filled nights, and one with a full moon. Reservations were required, and each visit would run for an hour. There was a free viewing available for everyone to see a quick sample of each program.

The Harold Seger Observatory was the other grand opening. It was named after the astronomer who had predicted the meteorite strikes years before they hit. Seger pleaded with officials to begin preparing immediately, but the country was embroiled in political strife, and there was little interest in extensive preparations for a possible scenario. The disaster, along with a series of catastrophic decisions, disintegrated what was left of the world's primary governments. The realization came too late, and the irreversible cascade of declining nations was initiated.

We were told the Harold Seger Observatory opening was scheduled for June 1, but sign-ups were open now. By late May, the shows were filling up. In the preview session, I attended with my school to watch the video narrated by our leading scientist on astronomy and meteorology. He described the drama of the powerful storms and cosmic events that would be displayed on the ceiling panels.

This was my third time in the Observatory, including our first day, the time with Gray, and now. Like then, the panels above rolled back to reveal the natural sky. Unlike the first time, the sky was filled with heavy clouds racing across the sky. I knew the sky was one of those things we must sacrifice to be safe, but I missed it.

In Denver, I spent time outside in my backyard and at the old park with GD and later Hayden. But I was always looking over my shoulder at the dangers lurking in the open. Back then, I viewed the night sky through dingy glass panes, but occasionally, we slipped into our backyard after curfew. Here, we had many more freedoms, but we were denied the sky.

I had enough credits to treat my family to an evening at the Observatory, so I got on my tablet and ordered four tickets for an evening show of a cosmic event. I sent my mom and dad a message stating the date and time. We decided to surprise Meshka.

At school that week, I started a study of caves. I gathered numerous articles on the types and geological events that caused them as well as the spelunkers who studied them. Two days into my program, I watched a video on cave mapping called cave cartography. Suddenly, I froze in my chair. Were my eyes betraying me? Was it that simple? My squiggly drawing clue didn't refer to a river after all. It was a cave map. But what cave? What territory, state, or country? If I had a clue which one, I'd run with my information to the town council, but my findings were woefully preliminary.

I listed off my mysteries in their various stages of discovery. I remembered and recorded the numbers on the sword scroll, but what did they mean? Was it the cave's location? Does Nitu Cabal lead to something that will help the rebels, and how do I read the invisible message under the desk? I knew something was amiss with the numerous attacks on Ari, Jilly, Zoey, and me. Those incursions must be part of this rebel movement because none of the leaders would talk about them honestly.

I would love to work with Rand on these clues. I was sure he had some of my missing pieces, and I knew I had some of his. But the time wasn't right yet. I feared the town leaders would dismiss my findings as a child's overreaching imagination while at the same time confiscating my work. I needed to continue my research, but at least now I had a direction. I planned to look up every cave map available.

Tensions were high since the Defenders died at the Hold. We worried we had been discovered despite the assurances to the contrary. It had been a particularly awful week. Two kids at school got into a fight about the attack, and both wanted me to justify their side.

They were yelling and posturing over who was to blame for Hannah's death. One blamed Gabe and the other blamed Gray. They weren't just Defenders to me. They were my friends. I felt both boys' arguments were founded in grief, based on opinions, and lacking enough facts to lay blame on either man. Unfortunately, the two boys fighting were Teke and Kato.

"There is no way they were trained well enough. Losing seven Defenders on one small mission?" yelled Teke. "Tell him, Connor, the guy in charge is responsible, and that's Officer Gray!"

"Yeah, but Officer Gabe was there!" shouted Kato. "He didn't read the situation right. They just blundered in. Officer Gray wouldn't do that, right Connor? I mean, you're close to both of them. What do you say?'

"You're both wrong!" I said charged with anger. "Gray and Gabe are highly trained. Most of those soldiers died before they got there. They didn't screw up, they were ambushed!"

"Oh yeah, well that just proves both of your friends suck, but I still say Officer Gray was in charge," Kato stated, pointing a mean scowl in my direction.

"You don't even address them correctly. If they're okay with letting a kid call them by nicknames and first names, it proves Officer Gray has let the discipline in his company slip!" Teke said, assuming an aggressive posture.

They were standing side by side now, aiming their fury at me. Teke and Kato were my friends, but so were Gray and Gabe. I couldn't let them belittle their sacrifice. I had to stick up for them.

"You both suck," I said. "Your arguments are stupid and cold-hearted. Why don't you try thinking through a problem for once, instead of throwing a tantrum about it?"

Teke shoved me, and I shoved back before Hayden, and another kid pulled us apart.

It went downhill from there.

Oddly enough, both Teke and Kato reclaimed their friendship through their shared disappointment in me. That would have been an acceptable outcome if it were anyone else. I knew it was our grief-ridden tempers releasing tension over our loss and the reality of the threat our town faced. We shared the same heartache, but instead of turning to each other, we turned against each other.

I was lucky I got to meet Hayden when we were forced to work together back in Denver. Most kids didn't get to have friendships. That experience helped me make more friends, and now I lost two of them. It left a horrible ache twisting in my core . The freedom to speak one's mind can spread joy and build nations, but it can also destroy as effectively as any weapon. I abused that power, and I didn't know how to walk it back.

I hoped leaving them alone would bring them around, but so far, their resolve stood strong. Though we didn't exchange any more hurtful words, glaring looks flew like daggers between us. If I were honest with myself, I wasn't ready to forgive them for what they said about my friends, who, by the way, were Hannah's friends too. I knew she wouldn't have blamed Gray and Gabe, and I also knew she wouldn't like how we were fighting. She'd want me to end it, but my pride blocked me from making a move.

Hayden tried to breach the divide by splitting his hangout time between us, but he was tired of the fray. So was I. I threw out a poorly worded apology only to have a new swarm of accusations come my way, which then triggered me to respond. We still had a lot of ammunition to pack up. The irony was that this little war had no purpose. It didn't change the outcome or honor our brave soldiers. It didn't make anything better. It just racked up more victims.

I was happy for the distraction when our Observatory date arrived. Although I had been getting a lot of time to work on my mysteries and schoolwork, everything felt muddled. I hadn't located any cave systems that came close to my map. There were too many holes in the clues I had to work with. My social life was in a painful state, and I missed my friends. I wished I could play baseball, but that required going to Wally's and not seeing Hannah behind the counter. Besides, who would I play with? I needed to look at the stars and relinquish my exaggerated significance.

When we walked into the round room, rows of lounge chairs encircled the space. Every seat offered a perfect view upward. The speaker welcomed and instructed us to stretch out our chairs as the huge dome doors rolled open. They rumbled down into the walls, revealing a clear window to the black night. It took a few seconds to adjust to the darkness before the stars started popping out one by one, filling the sky.

The speaker pointed out the dense river of stars sweeping across our view as the Milky Way, and he bounced his laser pointer off the transparent ceiling to identify the planets of our solar system as well as some constellations. He explained how sailors used the stars to travel the globe with little instrumentation. After about ten to fifteen minutes, he re-closed the doors, and the cosmic show began. The visual effect of traveling in space was so realistic that it made me dizzy, but I liked it. I had learned a lot about the solar system in school, but not like this.

At the end, he took questions and told us that new shows would be added as time went on. I could tell from the excitement of the attendees that it would take persistence to get tickets. I would come again. Maybe Hayden and I could get tickets to a severe weather program. The irony of watching a storm while being in the thick of one with my best friends was not lost on me.

When the show ended, Gray met my family on our way out and asked to speak to me for a moment. My parents left with Mesh. I wondered if he knew I was researching mysteries again from my map searches, and I wondered if he was going to tell me to stop. When everyone was gone, he told me to take a seat on one of the recliners. I heard the door close, leaving only us and the tense silence. What was he after?

"So, I know you know I gave Dewy Hannah's Rec Room job. He says he hasn't seen you. Not once."

I sat still for a while. "I just can't go in there and not see her."

"I get it. I have known Hannah since she was a kid hanging out with Axle. Those two were pledged like pirates and just as much trouble. It hurts every time I go into a safety meeting, or call Gabe for things I used to call her for, but she wouldn't want people to feel that way. And she'd hate that she caused you to stop playing ball."

"It's not just that," I sighed.

"I did hear there was some trouble with the fearsome four. Care to elaborate?"

He wasn't one to mince words. He was a straightforward guy, which I like about him. But the conversation was difficult for me because it involved him. I explained the fight and struggled through the part where he and Gabe were faulted. I began to go through my rant on their defense, but he stopped me.

"They have a right to their opinion, as do you. The topic is a tender one for sure. But that isn't the problem. You lack boundaries. When we are close to others, we hold them in high esteem. That gives them the power to make us feel good and be better people, but it also gives them the power to manipulate and hurt us deeply. That's how you know you care about them. If you didn't, it wouldn't hurt so much," he stared skyward, ending our eye contact, so I turned my face to the heavens too.

"How do you have an honest relationship with boundaries?" It seemed like the goals of friendship landed on the opposite end of having boundaries. Friendship was about being close and honest, while boundaries were about lines in the sand. I had a feeling this was going to be one of those conversations I would have to hash out in my head for days, weeks, maybe longer.

"Your pain comes from not understanding your friends' intentions. Were they just lashing out, or did they truly mean to hurt you? Regardless, they knew their statements would do that. Just like you knew calling them stupid would hurt them. That is what you need to clarify and then set some limits. It's not an easy task, but staying silent keeps you bruised indefinitely. It is hard not to get tangled up in the pain of one's past and the pertinacious pride they produce."

"Good alliteration, though somewhat forced," I snickered.

"I have my moments," he smiled. "But I have to admit, this is the same talk Haru had with me when Jilly and I were at odds. I'm borrowing his stuff."

"That makes sense. What was that fight about anyway? I mean, you saved her."

"That's what I mean about boundaries. That just isn't a conversation I'm going to share."

"Okay, but I'm a kid and you're an adult, so boundaries between us make sense. How do boundaries between you and your fiancé work? How do I manage them with my friends?"

"Look, I bet all three of your buddies know not to insult your grandad, right?"

"Yeah," I said, 'so what' running through my head.

"Well, you guys were all hurting and lashing out, but they still didn't hit that. It's a boundary they know. When the subject of Hannah came up, it would have been a good time to tell them it was too raw, too new, too painful. If they continued, it would have been better to walk away. Let the school deal with their shoving match. They got over it, but you took it personally. Hannah's death was a huge loss. Because we are also your friends, you felt you had to choose, meaning more loss. Maybe you didn't mean to lose more, but you did."

"Is that why you guys pummeled each other in the gym?" I wasn't sure if I was hitting one of his boundaries, but it seemed a little hypocritical that injuring each other didn't cross one.

"Yes, and no. The difference was, we weren't blaming each other. We were blaming ourselves, so there weren't any hard feelings afterward."

"What do I do? I tried to apologize, but I couldn't say they were right. They're not." I was feeling the ache of the emotions I had pushed down bubbling back up.

"It's not about right or wrong. It's about blame. Blame, especially in warfare with friends, is pointless. Learning is the key. My guess is they desperately want to repair the relationship they lost, but they are afraid to try. It's up to you. Go to them. Have a conversation saying you respect their right to have an opinion that differs from yours. Come to an understanding that your friendship is more important than deciding on a winner. Then, move on."

"You make it sound easy," I sighed.

"Oh no. It is far from that."

We reclined in the chairs for a while longer without saying a word. I tried to throw my woes at the stars, but they fell and settled back on me. It was time for the next show to start, so we made our way to the door.

CHAPTER 14

I was walking home alone the next day, having just finished tutoring Zoey. I was stewing over the fact that my three best friends were playing baseball without me. They had made the same plan on Tuesday, my other tutoring day. We had come to a rough peace, which included silence and avoidance. Hayden said I should join them after I was done, but it was unlikely they would continue to play after I arrived.

I might not get to play ball, but I decided it was time to try to repair the rift between us. I thought back to the knights' creed. Be brave, true, wise, gracious, and skilled. It was more than a list of noble words. It was a philosophy and a way to attack the issues life sends us. I had procrastinated talking with my friends for long enough. I worried that I would lose them forever if I spoke the wrong words, but I had already spoken the wrong words. At this point, all I had to lose was the dread of this conversation.

Hayden was hitting balls for them to field. I thought back to GD teaching me to throw and catch with that handmade ball he made from old leather shoes and the mitts made from his work gloves. I wish he could have lived to see this scene. The scene we fought for, and too many had died for. Our friendship was a part of that, and it was time to put it back together.

They all stopped when I walked out onto the field. Kato looked down, and Teke took a breath, bracing themselves for the unknown.

"Hi," I offered. My foes mumbled distant responses, but they all headed toward me.

"Finally, you made it to ball practice. Where's your mitt?" Hayden chided. By this time, Teke and Kato were standing with us in a circle.

"I've missed you guys. I want to get past this quarrel between us. I'm sorry I said those things. You have a right to believe in your conclusions. I wished I had kept my temper reeled in. It was a wild pitch, and I'm hoping we could...," Teke had a teary-eyed look, and he grabbed me into a hug.

"Shut up with the mushy stuff. Of course, we're friends. Bros over foes," Kato joined in with a punch to my shoulder.

"Bros over foes?" I asked.

"Yeah, my dad says something like that, but when I said it the way he does, my mom flicked my cheek," he said, rubbing the side of his head as if he could still feel the sting.

"It's a good motto," Hayden said. "We could say that before we start fighting."

"We're a team, and that's more important than any dumb quarrel," Teke agreed.

"We should make a pact to never let our differences divide us again. If one of us says that, we'll know an argument is getting too personal and heated. And if we don't stop, let's agree to walk away before we start firing hardballs at each other." I was happy that once more we were thinking alike.

Hayden put his hand over the top of the bat, and we all followed. "Agreed," we said as one.

"Now that the team's back together, let's play some ball!" yelled Teke.

Afterwards, I tried not to get overly emotional on my walk home, but I was so happy, it felt like my feet weren't touching the ground. I had dreaded that talk so much, and it turned out to be one of the best moments of my life. It was not nearly as hard as I imagined, and we even set some boundaries. Swallowing one's pride may be a big pill, but when it works out, it's the best medicine. *Thanks, Gray.*

When I got home, I pulled out those mitts and that old ball. I realized we not only saved our friendship today but maybe baseball too. We were the ones who made it happen, and the whole town was in now. Though volleyball was well attended, it wasn't nearly as popular as baseball had been. It was New Haven's first sport and part of our history.

I wrote a letter to Mr. Alex, the museum director, who I heard was working on a baseball exhibit. I offered these items, and he quickly responded with a resounding yes. I had such success with my friends that I decided it was time to introduce myself to Dewy.

Walking into Wally's, I saw a man with rumpled sandy hair and a seriously stubbled face sitting behind the counter. Hannah always popped right up when I came in. He looked up, but he stayed seated and greeted me by name.

"I've been waiting fer you ta come in, Connor," he said with a thick accent and a smile. He didn't look like a Defender to me. He continued to smile, but he didn't come around the counter or stand up to greet me properly. I wasn't sure that it qualified as unfriendly, but it didn't feel very welcoming either. I approached the counter and stopped. He was in a rolling chair with a fixture of some kind attached to his back. It brought new questions to mind. How could someone so ailing be a Defender?

"Dewy Quince," he said and winced as he reached his hand over the counter. I reciprocated the handshake, but I couldn't think of any words to say to him.

"Ya' should probably ask me about this chair, so we can get it over with," he said candidly.

"What happened?" was all I could come up with.

He went on to explain that he was on the mission with Hannah, and he was shot too. The bullet hit him in the back and paralyzed him, but he was undergoing treatment that should restore him completely. It was going to take a very long time before he could resume his regular Defender tasks, but he asked to work part-time at Walley's because this job had meant so much to Hannah.

Though he had a hydraulic device to assist him, I could see he struggled to lift his arms and retrieve the equipment. I surmised that shaving would be just as taxing, which explained the stubble. He said he worked four days a week, but he only had help on two.

"Did you know Hannah?" I asked, feeling my pain welling up.

"Very well. She is why I'm still alive," he said with a hitch in his voice.

"It's still hard," I said despite the swelling in my throat.

He bowed his head. I could see he had painful memories and deep sorrow. I wondered if he was reliving and rethinking what had happened that day. He cleared his throat and finally responded with, "Too hard sometimes," and turned his chair, pretending to attend to a task. I could see his pain went far deeper than the injury in his spine.

"I imagine you'll be needing these today," he said with a ball and glove in his hand. He had recomposed his tone and had his smile back on his face.

"No, today I thought I'd help at Wally's if you'll have me."

"It'd be an honor." He had a nice big smile that I looked forward to getting used to.

Friday was here, and I had been invited to spend the afternoon at the new beach in the Season Room with Mr. Vogel, Ellie, Savanah, Zoey, and Meshka. He invited me along to help since I had taken swimming lessons. I was excited to see it.

The lobby was the same, and we got the girls their swimming rings and went to the changing rooms. I had seen pictures of beaches, but I had no idea what to expect. Coming through the entry, I saw a pale sand-textured shore stretched out before us while large sandboxes flanked the edges of the beach area. Six people were already there, and we made twelve, which was close to the max, but it didn't feel crowded.

When the pool was here, there was a larger water area, but there was a generous amount of room on the beach to enjoy the warm sun lamps or play in the sandboxes on the sides. A light breeze swayed the fronds of the palm trees shading the sandcastle workers while waves rolled in a relaxing rocking motion.

The girls were watching the moving water, not sure how to approach it. I motioned for them to come forward, and I took two of their hands, and Mr. Vogel did the same for the other two. The water wasn't quite as warm as the pool had been, but the sun lamps heated the room, making the cool water feel refreshingly welcome. They finally made it out far enough to bob on their rings, causing surprised giggles.

I lay back and floated, enjoying the wave motion rocking me to and fro in a weightless state. I had heard real ocean waves were rough and dangerous, but someday I'd like to see the real ocean and float in it.

I liked Mr. Vogel, but he had a commanding presence, which I found intimidating, but the silence was becoming awkward.

"So, Mr. Vogel, how is Ari doing?" I asked. I knew they were engaged, and the group wedding day was approaching.

"How about you call me Mr. V.? It feels less stuffy to me," he said. "To answer your question, she's doing well. I am very fond of her."

"I have noticed that. She's a good catch, as Dewy would say." I suddenly hoped I hadn't overstepped my boundaries by joking around like that.

But he laughed. "Good man, Dewy. I hear you've been helping him at Wally's. I appreciate that. I'll make sure you get credits for your time."

"You don't have to do that, Mr. V., I'm helping him because I like him, and Hannah would want me to be there for him."

"Just the same," he said, "your work is worth a wage, and I have all this stuff in the barrier just waiting for buyers."

"Why did you build all these over-the-top amenities? I mean, most of the residents had no idea these things could exist. They would have been happy with food, shelter, and safety. They never would have missed all this."

"Well," he started, "I got most of these things for nothing because, as you so aptly put it, no one saw a need for them. The Corporates bought some, but there were warehouses of things like this, and being a shipping and supply business, I ended up with a lot of dumped goods. Everyone thought I was crazy to keep all this junk, but there is a barrier of thousands of shipping containers surrounding both entrances to this town, and every one of them is filled to the brim with supplies.

"I even have supplies for trading if we find allies on the outside. And nothing is so singular in its purpose that it can't be utilized for other needs. The only items I worry about running out of are the medicinal ones. Some ingredients are very difficult to come by, and many have a limited shelf life. But our Dr. is top-notch, and she's working with Raff O'Leary to engineer lab equipment that can make synthetic copies."

"Thank you for all you have given us, Mr. V. We are very lucky to live here. I wish everyone could live this way. If they did, they would do anything to keep it going and defend it."

"That's the idea, Connor. I believe that if people see what is possible, they will strive for it, they will stand up to anyone trying to take it, and they will fight for it like you fought for baseball."

It was nice to get to know Mr. V. better. He always seemed so unapproachable that I didn't feel comfortable around him, but that changed today.

CHAPTER 15

On Tuesday, I met Zoey as usual. I could have ended her lessons over a month ago because she had more than caught up with her studies, but I enjoyed teaching her, and she asked me to stay on as her tutor. She was still shy and anxious with people, but we had a candid demeanor, so I concluded she still needed a mentor. I know what it is like to hide a big secret alone, and I was determined to unravel what happened to her mother and her aunt in a way that didn't involve hurting her. The New Haven Memorial Wall seemed like the perfect opportunity.

The tribute took time to finish, but it took me more time to feel ready to view it. I figured Zoey was also apprehensive, so I thought we would visit it for the first time together. I knew it would be emotional to see Hannah's name up there, but it was time to pay my respects. When we turned down the corridor where the memorial was placed, Zoey got nervous.

"Zoey, what's going on? We are just going to see your mom's name. It will be okay." I grabbed her hand.

"What if my aunt's name is on there? Everyone will know, and I can't talk about it."

"If it scares you, you should talk about it. Have you seen Haru?" We were stopped in front of the corridor that led to the wall.

"Yes," she said softly. "He says nothing bad will happen anymore and none of it was my fault. I mean, they looked so much alike that everyone thought she was my mom. But I knew she wasn't. She looked bad and talked mean, not like my mom."

"What happened to your mom?" I asked, knowing I was invading her don't-tell realm.

"She got sick after Merita showed up. My mom said she didn't know she had a sister, but she found us somehow. At first, I thought she was being nice and taking care of my mom. My mom worked at a dental clinic, so when she got sick, her boss gave her medicine to get better. I saw Merita taking my mom's medicine and giving her different pills. My mom got worse and worse."

"Merita was your aunt?" They must have been twins, I thought. It was common to separate twins at birth because of the suspicions surrounding them. People thought they were possessed or ill because they were often sickly and sometimes deformed. To keep them from being killed along with their families, the Corporates let the parents keep one, and they took the other to a childless couple. They were all about making sure they had a steady stream of future workers.

"I wasn't supposed to say that," she answered. "But I trust you. My mom's name was Marni. When she died, Merita said she hid her body, so we could still come here. She pretended to be her, so we could get in here. But they found the ring and figured out it wasn't her. She dragged me and pulled my hair. She was trying to get outside. Didn't she know it was too cold? I think her brain was sick."

I knew now her aunt was a toxer. She abused toxic waste, which is very addictive, to get high. She found her sister and undoubtedly caused her illness, so she could steal her drugs and her money, allowing her to acquire more from local dealers. She must have thought she won the mother lode when she discovered her sister had a job as a dental assistant and a ticket to New Haven with access to a plethora of strong medicine. I'm not sure how a ring gave her away, but poor Zoey had been caught in the crossfire.

"What happened to your aunt?"

"Dewy and Axle caught her and saved me. I haven't seen her since, but Mr. V said she was in jail."

Interesting, I thought. She was jailed without a trial. So somewhere we have a jail here in New Haven. I don't remember that being on the tour. The handbook says all residents get a trial. Maybe they didn't consider her a resident. She could have been viewed as a combatant because she scammed her way in for nefarious reasons. I doubted there was a jail for combatants, and I also doubted we'd see Merita's name on the wall. Though the mystery of her aunt's whereabouts was unsolved, I knew the seriousness of this secret.

"Come on Zoey, let's go see your mom's name."

The names were parked in neat rows on a field of darkly stained wood, under the phrase: *Forever remembered with gratitude and honor*. A row of soft lights illuminated each panel. The names were arranged by the date of death. We began our walk by six empty frames silently waiting for the next additions. They displayed their nothingness with the ominous reality of our impending mortality.

As I glanced down the corridor, I could see the plaques filled with more names than I expected. Their lifespans were etched on small brass plates and inked in black. The first names were of the soldiers we had recently lost at the Hold. I found Hannah's nameplate, and I passed my finger over the etching, feeling the texture of it. It was cold and still, but it honored her.

Just above Hannah, we found Marni, but Merita was nowhere to be seen. Zoey had a sad expression.

"I miss her so much. It makes me sad that people will think my mean aunt was my mom. They probably didn't like her, but they would have."

"We know, Zoey. And so do Dewy, Axle, and others."

We moved down the wall back in time, passing many names of people who helped make New Haven happen but didn't make it here. Just then, another name caught my eye: Deegan Chance.

"Oh, look Zoey! It's my grandad." I had told her many stories about him, and she smiled.

"I'm glad we came. Now every time I pass, I'll tell my mom she made it here because she's inside my heart. And you can say that about GD too." I smiled and gave her a side hug as she leaned her head into me.

"I'm glad too. I've told you so many stories about GD. Tell me about your mom." Once she started, the precious moments she had hidden away flowed like a spring creek. She didn't notice when I extended our walk as, one by one, she culled the cobwebs and revived her happy memories.

Another new person came into my life around that time. Zoey would always be dear to me, but her need for a tutor had gone well past its time. She had advanced to the next grade with her friends, and I was needed somewhere else. Sandra was a high school student. She had experienced something traumatic just before she came to the Hold and lost her hearing. The doctors could not find a physical reason for her hearing loss, so they assumed it was due to the trauma of her experience.

In the outside world, workers with defects were not tolerated. Well-planned accidents, disappearances, or public removals of such persons were common. As a result, society had lost its ability to accommodate handicaps. She had been learning sign language on her own from computer files, but it was time consuming for her and difficult for her teachers to master effectively. They depended on the tablet to communicate, but it was clumsy and frustrating for all involved.

I was chosen because of my eidetic memory. I picked up sign language easily, and I was able to extend her skills until our communication was more than just effective; it was engaging. I became the only person she could talk to with ease. I decided to learn how to read lips and teach her. I believed it would be more helpful to her in a non-signing community. It has limitations if the speakers' faces aren't in view or don't enunciate well, but it is better than the other, more awkward means of communication. What I didn't count on was how useful this skill could be to my investigations. It was beyond invasive, but I found it difficult to turn away sometimes.

I discovered more things about my community than I had wanted to. My neighbor, Melody, had a crush on Noah and was planning to sit in the back row at the movies and kiss him. Another woman ranted about not being allowed to cook her own meals. I saw a kid being scolded by his parents for the serious act of stealing, and then they defended him to those he wronged.

There were funny moments too. It was discovered that April First was a day when people used to play pranks on each other. Two kids confessed to putting balloons under a cart, making the startled driver pull over and walk around checking the tires. Another printed off bug stickers and put them all over their diner. A couple thought their friend was too slow to ask his girlfriend to marry him, so they snuck a toy ring into her drink to prompt the conversation. They're engaged now and will be married in July.

The most disturbing lesson I learned is how quickly people change their attitudes about an issue depending on who they're talking to. Parents would frown and scold children who misbehaved and then laugh about the incidents among other adults. People say they're upset with others and turn around and engage with them, showing no sign of concern.

I couldn't unlearn the skill, but I needed to develop more discipline in using it. It's a good thing I'm experienced at keeping secrets.

Sandra was a shy girl with big dark eyes and hair the color of midnight. Since she had been born with hearing, she could speak relatively well. We used sign language at first, and she was surprised when my ability surpassed her own within a week. She seemed to come back to life with me being her voice, and I liked the way she expressed herself. She was mysterious, witty, moody, and flirtatious all at once. Being one of the few people she could communicate with, we spent a lot of time together.

I had been dedicated to Zoey, and I happily devised ways to teach her new concepts. Sandra had my dedication too, and I eagerly devised reasons to spend more time with her. I loved little Zoey, and I felt protective of her. When she hugged me, it was like hugging my little sister. I had strong feelings for Sandra, and I felt possessive of her. When she hugged me, it wasn't like hugging my sister.

She had above-average intelligence, and she was picking up lip reading quickly, but we still used sign language or the tablet for difficult words and concepts. I made a lot of concessions to make her comfortable around me, like hiding my intellect and my feelings. Although the necessity to hide my Highmind status was gone, it was a private part of me that I chose to keep to myself. It made people feel at ease when I talked casually without broadcasting my knowledge or using specific vocabulary. We were talking about the up-and-coming weddings when she said something that I'll never forget.

"You know Connor," Sandra said, killing me with her flirty head tilt, "no one understands me like you do. Not even my parents can talk to me with the ease that we do. You're so smart, but not obnoxious smart. You're interesting and cute," she added coyly. "I can tell you will be handsome when you grow up. Sooo," she stretched the word, "I guess I'm just going to have to marry you," and she kissed me on the cheek.

I could feel the heat rise on my face, and I laughed nervously like it was a joke. But it wasn't a joke, not to me. It was a dream come true. She was perfect for me, and she just admitted I was perfect for her. I wanted it so badly that I believed that at eleven, almost twelve, a girl of sixteen would want to be my girlfriend. I lived on those words, and if I'm honest, I still do, a little, because she was my first love, and I fell hard.

It was no surprise that single adults had found partners in our little town. After all, I met Sandra. Arranged marriages were a thing of the past since women were safe from both aggressive authorities and protective parents. Multiple weddings were to be held at one grand ceremony the first week of July. Jilly and Ari were both going to be among those brides.

What shocked the community was that after nine months of being locked in the tunnel, the group ceremony and reception might be held outside. Every honest resident had to admit they missed the open skies and mountain air. However, the safety of the town depended on our mountaintop appearing abandoned. Many were frightened to go outside and worried about the satellites that circled the earth searching for any sign of deviations or unsanctioned activity.

To calm the rising concerns, a news report explained the allowance. A group of anti-technology rebels, called No-Techys, purposely set in motion something called the Kessler Syndrome. They hacked into defense satellites and strategically destroyed many of the surveillance satellites orbiting our planet. They targeted them so they would send out as much shrapnel as possible, creating a chain reaction of destruction. Over time, it turned the outer layers of our atmosphere into a debris field in a perpetual mode of self-annihilation.

Corporate drones were large, slow, and flew on predictable schedules, giving us a window of freedom. But without overhead visuals of the atmosphere, determining the weather was back to old-school instruments. The threat was small, which seemed to satisfy most residents, but a few were still in conspiracy mode, thinking we had been tricked. I was more excited about being outside than I was worried. I couldn't believe the leaders would risk the town for a walk in the sunshine.

More news was shaking up our small town. Seven unplanned pregnancies and the six newlywed couples required a shift in the housing. New Haven had quite a few empty houses in expectation of a growing population, but it counted on slow growth. The best news was that Jilly and Gray would remain in her two-bedroom house, so I wouldn't lose my neighbor.

We also had more Defenders from the offsite stations. I was glad to have more soldiers, but it required additional housing shifts. A large Defender dorm was built so recruits could be billeted there, and the older single Defenders would move into remodeled group homes.

I had been tutoring Sandra for two months when she had a breakthrough at one of her sessions with Haru. Her hearing was returning. It was sporadic, but Haru was confident her hearing would soon return completely. The time she used to spend with me was now spent with Haru, meaning her need for a tutor had ended. I should be happy for her, but I wasn't. I knew. She didn't need me anymore. She was still nice to me, but our previous closeness dwindled into awkward company. Still, I clung to hope she cared about me as I did her, denying the painful truth that stabbed at my heart.

CHAPTER 16

I saw Gray and Rand sitting in one of the diners, and they motioned me over. While I hooked Libby to the fence, they took the opportunity to end their discussion. I know I shouldn't read their lips, but I couldn't help it when I realized they were talking about a place, a place called Cali Bantu.

The last thing they said was that they had come to a dead end in finding its location. When I walked back to the table, the conversation quickly changed to the approaching basketball season.

"Hey, it's been a while," I said quietly. He dressed me down like the thorough Defender he is.

"Whoa, who stole your sunshine?" He's good. I'll give him that. I was regretting standing before him with my heart bleeding agony all over the place.

"Aw, I'm just feeling a little off. I guess I'm bored since baseball ended, and I don't have any students to tutor." I was getting sadder by the minute.

Rand gave me a concerned look. "Even I know better, and I suck at human stuff."

I swallowed hard. I never should have stopped. Gray picks up on everything. "Are you having girl trouble already?" he asked.

"You know, O.G.," I said seriously, shortening the respectful title he deserved, "maybe you should mind your own business." My defensive hackles were raised, and all the hurt and anger I was feeling suddenly had a target. I was feeling bad about my ill-gotten clue and contemplating my ethics. But now I turned toward decoding that clue right then and there.

It wasn't much of a stretch; Cali Bantu unscrambled was Nitu Cabal. I decided to spend every second finding its location before them. They probably didn't know it was a cave. So there, I thought, puffing up a bit. Dig into my secrets, and I'll beat you at yours. Gray turned and raised an intimidating eyebrow at my brazen reply and visible attitude.

"Whoa," Rand chuckled, trying to defuse the snowball of tension heading toward them. "Look at his face. It *is* girl trouble. He's got a crush, and it's going wrong."

Officer Gray took a breath and nodded his head. "You know why they call it a crush, Connor? It is what young love does to your heart." I slumped into the chair at the table. "Wow, you need some bro time. Have you told your friends?" I shook my head no. "Well, they're pretty young, but they might understand. You have to go through it to know how much it burns. But I've had my share of heartbreaks, and I'll listen."

"Yeah, bros before hoes," said Rand. "That's what guys say, and then they plan a drinking night, and..."

"Rand! Chill out. He's eleven!" said Officer Gray. "Seriously, Connor, even if you were older," Gray gave Rand an admonishing look, "drinking doesn't cure a bad mood. It turns it into a monster. Talking about it works better. What happened Connor? We're all ears."

"Yeah, I want to hear too. I can get first dates, but I don't get second ones," said Rand.

I paused to consider Rand for a moment. He was so smart, but he tried too hard to fit in. I wondered if, I showed my intellect if this was what my life would look like, alone and awkward. If I were honest, I already felt that way. I had hidden my Highmind status from Sandra, but she must have known my intelligence was above normal since I could instruct her on high school studies.

I was dying to tell someone what she did, someone who would take my experience seriously, someone who would be on my side, and someone who had a cure for the ache drilling through the very core of me. I hoped I had the right audience. I bared my soul, and besides the occasional question, they let me finish the whole tale, well my side anyway.

"Yeah, she led you on," Gray said. "She's still young too. She just wanted to try out her power and see how it worked. You were a safe test subject because she trusted you not to act on her advances. I doubt she realizes how much she hurt you. It sounds like you knew it was a long shot, but you stayed the course. It's like watching a severe storm through your window. Your brain says turn away, but you stand there mesmerized by the drama of it. You don't think about that fragile wall of glass until reality comes crashing through it."

"What do I do? I thought it would fade, but every day feels worse."

"Well, if you're okay with just being friends, you could talk with her. But it's unlikely she will see your side. I would avoid her. She might say things that hurt you to justify her actions, or she may want to tangle you back up because it makes her feel powerful. I'd say, walk away. It will take a while, but the hurt will fade. In the meantime, hang out with your friends. You have three solid allies. Do what you love. Baseball comes to mind. Or maybe, you should try your hand at basketball. Committing to all those practices will fill your days and wear you out."

"Is it true there is only one true love for everyone? Was that it for me?" I heard the hitch in my voice as I spoke.

"I can answer this one," said Rand. "The statistical odds of finding your soulmate are one in a thousand, and most people fall in love an average of three times. But that study was done before the Big Strike, and we don't have the same freedom to meet people, sooo…"

"Rand, is that one of the things you say on those first and consequentially last dates?" Gray shook his head. "Math and love don't live in the same dimension. You're eleven, Connor. Slow down. This girl came into your life organically. That's how it works best." He got a grin on his face and said, "Oh yeah, and I like the nickname, O.G. You have permission to use it, without the attitude," He said, pointing his finger and sending me a warning glare. I smiled and gave him a thumbs-up. I was feeling a bit better after hanging out and talking with them.

"So, is now the time to get ice cream?" asked Rand.

"Yep, I think so," said Gray, "my treat."

This weekend would keep me busy. I had inventory work at Wally's, the weddings were this Saturday, and on Sunday Alex wanted me to help with the baseball exhibit. I should also set up a meeting to confess what I had discovered, especially since they had hit a dead end.

Saturday arrived, and everyone was excited to be outside. We stood in line waiting to walk through the large freight doors and into the outside world. The cool air hit my face as soon as the doors were pushed open. It was refreshing, and I breathed it in deeply. The weather cooperated, sending friendly cumulous clouds floating across a blue sky. I forgot how bright and invigorating the real sky was. What we had in the tunnel was amazing, but just like love, it was better when it was organic.

We were on the west side of the tunnel facing a horseshoe barrier of shipping containers, three high and two thick. It looked like a fortress. I was told the east entrance was similar but much smaller. Four well-dressed grooms waited in front of the audience for their brides to come down the aisle. Bannon had an Italian suit from his days of traveling for business. Gray wore his black dress uniform with a white button-up shirt.

The chatting crowd stopped when the music began to play. The first bride came out and stood by her groom, and next came Ari. She had an elegant sleeveless white dress. It was a classic style accented with a sparkling pendant necklace.

Jillian was the last bride to walk out of the tunnel. She wore a white dress that came to her knees in the front and went to the floor in the back. The sleeveless bodice ended at the thin black belt, and an A-line skirt of light material flowed around her legs. A row of black lace encircled the inside of the high-low hemline, creating a striking contrast where it was exposed. I wondered where they got such nice clothes, but then I looked at the countless shipping containers surrounding us.

Haru spoke of love, wisdom, and enduring marriages. He used the metaphor of a ship on a sea to describe a relationship. He said that couples had to become good navigators and be each other's loyal crew in stormy weather. I thought of the smashed window metaphor O.G. described, and I wondered if it was worth it. Jilly and Gray had been through difficult times, but were they closer in spite of it or because of it?

I saw Sandra talking with a boy her age. It was amazing how quickly she regained her voice and confidence. I wondered if it was worth talking to her. She probably didn't even know there was a problem, and it was plain to see she wasn't willing to weather any kind of storm for me. If I talked to her, then what? Would we become friends? Was that good enough? Would I be happy for her when she started dating someone else? No, Gray was right. I needed to let her go. I turned away. I didn't want to see her give that coy smile to this boy, the one she used to give to me.

Gray, Axle, and Gabe donated elk meat for the meal, and it was bar-bequed to perfection. We even had a live band with four musicians. The live music energized the crowd to dance under the boundless sky. With the help of the band, Gray played his guitar and sang a song to Jillian. Bannon announced that he and Ari were expecting a baby in the fall. The day was flooded with happy news, but it spilled out of me as fast as it poured in.

The town purchased a honeymoon hour for each couple to be alone at the beach scene. I donated the credits I earned at Wally's. Normally, twelve to fifteen people could enjoy the beach, so getting it to themselves was a real treat.

I hadn't seen Axle since Hannah died, so I decided to say hi. He was intercepted by a woman, so I hung back and waited. They were dancing, and I was trying not to watch them, so I couldn't inadvertently eavesdrop on their conversation. But I could tell they had some sort of disagreement because suddenly Axle stopped dancing and stepped away from her. He was as mad as I had ever seen him. He quickly strode away to lean on the wall at the edge of the barrier. I decided to connect with him later.

It started to sprinkle, and it was reported that the light rain would soon turn into a full storm. The wedding was winding down, and a call was made to return to the tunnel. I watched as one of the new Defenders walked toward Axle, still hanging at the edge of the barrier. She wound through the crew packing carts with chairs, tables, and flower pots decorating the grounds. She was working security at the wedding, and I couldn't look away from the conflict that was about to happen.

She stopped a good distance from the cornered lone wolf, and a stare-down commenced. I assume she told him to retreat, but I could only see her back. Axle didn't move. He stood ready to defend his corner. She started using gestures and slowly walking toward him, encouraging him to head in. Reluctantly, he left the wall and walked toward the door, jerking his jacket as if it irritated him. The move was a warning of his raw mood, but she challenged him back by standing her ground. *What did the woman he danced with say to make him so angry?* He walked past the patrolling Defender without making eye contact.

It was a mystery for sure, but it was his, and it was no doubt a personal one. I know how painful relationships can be, and I also knew he needed time to work it out.

CHAPTER 17

Today was my meeting at the museum with Alex Walker. It was closed to the public while we rotated the exhibits. We were setting up a baseball exhibit, including my old equipment. I would earn three credits, which I planned on adding to my scooter fund. They cost forty credits, and so far I had twelve.

Credits are hard to come by, especially for kids. The rate for my age was one credit per hour. Kids were only allowed to volunteer six hours a week, but participation in sports also earned credits, two a week. I earned the max when I played ball, tutored, and worked at Wally's. Now I only work at Wally's. Maybe Dewy would let me up my hours, or I'll get another student. Regardless, today I'd be three credits closer.

"Hi, Mr. Walker. I brought the mitts and balls. My dad hand-carved a bat for me, but we had to leave it in Denver. We couldn't transport it to Fairplay." He nodded in understanding. I handed him the ball first.

"Your grandad was a master craftsman," he said, taking it gently from my hand and turning it to see all sides. "Look at the stitching on this ball, and it's about as round as it can be even after all the use it suffered." He was fawning over the abused ball, admiring the sheen from shoe leather oil and the hands that threw it during its second life.

"Yeah, we threw it as often as we could, and I used it to teach Hayden how to play after GD died. I'm sure you'll want to clean it. It's kind of nasty."

"Well, it's a shame I have to clean it, but only enough to preserve it. The dirt is part of its charm, its history. It demonstrates its place in the story to save something important. It is a symbol of your quest for freedom. You know baseball was referred to as the chess game of physical sports because it is layered with complex strategies."

"But chess is a game of war," I said, though I remembered Hannah making the same connection before our championship game.

"Ahh," he said, pointing upward, "and what sport isn't a re-enactment of that?" His eyes sparkled as he spoke.

I pulled out the repurposed work gloves, and a similar response was expressed, bestowing great value on them too. He was reverent when he held the weathered objects, demonstrating his appreciation. His words gave a voice to what I thought each time I held them. I'm glad I donated them. New Haven now had a record of baseball's return, and my treasures were in the care of someone who cherished them as much as I did.

I wondered if the residents might dismiss it as junk now that we had been spoiled with so many new things. I remembered the days of finding useful discarded items with delight. I knew all too well how one's circumstances dictated one's perspective. It transformed trash into treasure, and in here that transformation was applied to people. GD said that remembering where we came from is how we find where we belong. That is the purpose of museums.

The display cases were moved upstairs using the small elevator, along with the items going inside. I figured we could make quick work of settling everything in its place, but I was wrong. Alex, who insisted I call him that, was meticulous in the handling of the items in his care.

I learned things about baseball I never knew. The first players used homemade equipment, like I did. I wondered if GD knew that and used those patterns from a leftover era. Knowing him, my guess was he did. The sport took hold in the 1830's and by the 1950s, the first ball clubs were formed.

Three large books that were set on a counter caught my attention. The books contained pictures, articles, and hundreds of baseball cards, all secured inside clear shiny sleeves. Two of the books focused on the Hall of Famers like Mickey Mantle, Hank Aaron, Ken Griffey Jr., and Joe DiMaggio. The other one included fascinating stories about those who broke the exclusive barriers and made history like Ichiro Suzuki, Shoeless Joe Jackson, and Roberto Clemente.

The most tragic player was the one on the last page. He wasn't on anyone's best-player list, but he was the last one. His name was Grant Collier, but they called him the Preacher.

He tried to bring back baseball in New York after the meteorite dust had settled. Baseball was the sport that defined us early in the United States, and he thought reviving it would re-energize our patriotic desire for freedom. He went against the Corporate masters making their play for ultimate control. At what was to be the final game, he stood on the pitcher's mound and addressed the small crowd brave enough to come. The newly formed Neighwah army gunned him down on that mound, and everyone ran out of the dilapidated stadium never to return.

We stood back and eyed the exhibit. There were pictures, trophies, famous game balls, uniforms, and a video screen playing notable moments we could hear on our earbuds. The display cases gave value to the pieces and honored the memories they shared. The inviting arrangement flowed nicely from one piece to the next. I needed to move to my next task, but I'd return and spend time with those books.

I was bringing out the display cases and tables when Fin and Brook, Mr. Alex's assistants, came up the stairs. They announced they were ready to get the *Egyptian* and the *Geological Meteorite Wonders* exhibit pieces from the storage room. Alex handed them the key saying he would be right there. I was conflicted about the positive connection to the meteorite disaster.

As we were sliding the crates off the hand truck, I decided to ask. "Why are you using *'Wonders'* to describe meteorites? I mean, *Wonders* doesn't seem like the best way to describe what happened. It destroyed everything," I said, hoping I didn't offend him.

"Earth's destructive forces have always caused hardships for this planet's inhabitants, but they also created the most incredible land formations. They unlock Earth's most guarded secrets, and they are part of our story. Have you studied much geology in school?"

Studying geology certainly did help me understand my map, and such formations were protecting an important secret. "Yeah, we just finished a lesson on caves. I will admit they are beautiful and interesting. Volcanoes give an impressive show and shape some extraordinary landscapes. But this event happened so recently and ended everything. I think too much gloom surrounds it for people to see it as a wonder."

"True," said Alex solemnly. "The meteorites caused the death of half the human population. If we had heeded Harold Seger's warning, we would have had years to prepare, and many more people would have survived. People need to see what the forces of nature are capable of, so they will heed such warnings with reverence.

"Even when it was a certainty, those with authority sought to secure their power before the safety of the people. What civilization is living through now is due to our lack of humanity, not meteorites." I couldn't argue with that. I still didn't want to stand face to face with depictions of the tragedy that rocked our world off its game, so I waved goodbye knowing his staff was waiting for him.

A nightly news report was presented by a group of innovative high school students, and I made a point of watching it. They didn't report the outside information, but to my knowledge, we received very little of that. Yet, I enjoyed learning about our citizens' accomplishments, needs, and the plans from city council. They were the ones who conveyed the news of the Kessler Syndrome which destroyed most of the satellites.

Tonight's report concentrated on the town's solution to our loss of surveillance. Since we could no longer rely on satellites to monitor the area around the tunnel, two teams were being sent out to set up relay stations containing reconnaissance drones. It worried me to hear that another offsite mission was scheduled. The last time our Defenders went offsite, they were attacked, resulting in seven dying and Dewy being so seriously injured, he was still recovering.

I had always known the Defenders' job was to face danger, but losing Hannah brought that frightening reality to the forefront. When the two teams' pictures were displayed, I was further alarmed to see Axle was one of them. It also did not escape my attention that he was partnered with the Defender, who ordered him to retreat into the tunnel. Both showed they could be quite intimidating and tenacious. I guess that's what made them good warriors, but it would probably make for a very long trip.

They were scheduled to leave the next morning, so I got up early to see Axle before school. I went to the security building hoping I could catch him before he took off. I never had the chance to say anything to Hannah before she left on her last and fatal mission. I didn't want to repeat that regret. He was walking with determined intensity, wrestling with the gear flung over his back.

"Axle," I shouted, "wait."

He paused. "I'm kind of in a hurry, Connor. What did you need?"

He was radiating powerful energy, and I almost lost my nerve. "I just, um, I just wanted to wish you a safe journey."

His mood softened considerably. No words were needed to communicate his complete understanding of my intent. "I know you're worried because of what happened last time. This mission is not as hazardous. We are staying off the beaten path to hide drone stations. There is little chance we'll see troops in Fringer territory, or any Fringers for that matter. But I'll be careful."

"Well, my wish is that everything goes well. And I hope you and your partner keep each other safe."

He laughed at that and said, "That's good advice, Connor. I'll take it." He waved as he headed to the door. I wasn't good at praying, but I said one.

I thought about what he said about Fringers. Dailys were taught to be afraid of Fringers. Fringers were tribes of deserting soldiers and escaped criminals who lived on the fringes of the territories. Though little was known about them, they were blamed for all sorts of isolated crimes on Dailys and our border, but they weren't seen as organized or well-armed. The Defenders were more of a threat to them.

A week went by, and I still hadn't made it back to the museum. I took Gray's advice and joined a basketball team. Unlike baseball, basketball was a contact sport. I went home with more bruises and scratches caused by other players as opposed to stray balls and sliding on the ground.

Although I wasn't one of the best players, I excelled at the point guard position because I could dribble the ball well. I loved the fast pace of the game and its high-scoring aspect. It was a change from the slower pace of baseball with its complex strategies. Though I liked the spontaneity of basketball, baseball remained my favorite.

Outside, it was the middle of summer, and the residents were again allowed to go out of the tunnel, but not all at once. We took turns attending the activities that had been set up for us. My family and Hayden's had remained close, and we were allowed to go out at the same time. A game called miniature golf was set up on one side of the yard, and a go-cart track was on the other. Hayden and I qualified to drive go-carts after a short training session.

I had never driven anything before, and I didn't think to ask after a high schooler got in trouble for jumping on one and crashing it into a resident's fence. But driving was a blast. I could almost understand his impulsiveness. The track had safety rails, and the carts weren't very fast, but Hayden and I maxed them out the whole ride trying to squeal around the turns.

Our little sisters weren't old enough to drive the carts, but we played a game of miniature golf with them. I was surprised that Meshka held her own against us ball-batting champs. We were treated to hamburgers, barbeque beans, potato chips, and ice cream. Another amazing day in New Haven.

I was exhausted and slept until my mom woke me up to go to my basketball game the next morning. It was a close game, but we lost by three. With only two teams in my age group, we weren't having a championship contest, but the last game was coming up. The other team had one win over us, and it would be a tough competition.

That night I sat on my bed watching the nightly report. A shocking crime involving a very sensitive issue was reported, and it involved Dewy and the woman Axle danced with at the wedding. Her name was Tanya, and she attacked Dewy. She wanted a baby, but he refused to go behind the planning commission, so she drugged him.

"She realized the error of her plan when Dewy fell while fighting her. He was taken to the medical facility where they said he suffered minor damage to his spinal injury, but he would recover. New Haven's first criminal trial was to be held in two weeks," the report said in conclusion. I wondered if she asked Axle the same thing and that's what caused him to get so angry.

Tanya's trial brought out the activists in droves. Some wanted leniency, others suggested counseling, and some wanted her jailed. One extremist wanted her executed. I was still curious about the location of our jail. Unlike Merita, who knew something so dangerous that she had to disappear, Tanya would have a public trial. It was our first serious criminal trial.

The next day was Sunday, and I went to the museum to finally spend some time in the baseball book. As I walked through the doors, I was shocked by a painting front and center in the *Geological Meteorite Wonders* exhibit. It was of a gouged-out mountainside. The exposed earth was red and raw while the sky boiled with orange dust clouds. Flames demonstrated the newness of Earth's injury, and the wound revealed a great cavern where something glowed from within.

I knew this painting. I had seen it before. I was only a toddler when my grandad showed it to me. I walked over and looked at the signature, A.T., scripted on the bottom. It was too close to Alec T., or ALECT, to be a coincidence.

"This is important, Connor. Remember it," I recalled GD telling me that. Could this be the mountain that held the secret cave? Could this be Cali Bantu?

I needed to hold back my excitement. If I said something, they might take it and run without me, and that could end up in disaster. I know they wanted to protect me because of my age, but I held important knowledge of this Cali Bantu, and finding it was just the beginning.

CHAPTER 18

We were well into August, and our basketball season was over. Although I was disappointed my team lost the final game by a last-minute layup, it was a close competition the whole season. I had no regrets. I did, however, lose the two credits a week for participating in a team sport. I returned to tutoring students twice a week for test prep, and I still spent two days a week at Wally's. Gray was right that keeping busy was the ticket to letting Sandra go.

I had worked tirelessly to find the mountain in the painting, hoping it was the location of Cali Bantu. Assuming the mountain was hit by a meteorite and the painting was a true depiction of how it was damaged, finding it would be difficult using pictures of post-meteorite geography. I should contact Gray to tell him what I knew, but I didn't feel ready. I needed a way to ensure I wouldn't be left out of further research.

The Defender teams sent to improve our surveillance capabilities returned, but Axle's team required a month of quarantine. I was dying to talk with him about the adventure. I also wondered what they ran into that required a month of isolation.

Next month would mark the first anniversary of living in New Haven. Although the residents had settled into the town in several stages, the official date was marked by the closing of the doors. That's when my group arrived. It was dizzying to think of all that had happened in a single year.

It was a stark difference from our lives under Corporate rule, which passed at a steady, albeit dreary tempo interrupted only by tragedies.

First, we moved to higher elevations, and before we had time to settle in, we were transported to the Hold. There we lived in a large warehouse separated by canvas walls and forced to interact with each other every day. It was awkward at first, but with guidance, we found harmony in the warmth of fellowship. Though a year had passed, most of us still dealt with the leftover issues of our enslavement, but not as often. I put my trust in this environment soon after arriving. Why wouldn't I? It was the world my grandad spoke of. That trust was damaged when I was abducted, and it is still surrounded by mysteries.

But time has worked its magic, and most people are now enjoying their surroundings. People have found their voice and educated themselves in the political freedoms they now have. Our town settled into a blissful rhythm of freedom and security.

I hoped I never see the day that these privileges and rights are taken for granted. Democracy isn't a promise; it takes work and sacrifice. Many great nations before us forgot that and perished, and now the concept is being erased and on the verge of extinction. As far as we knew, we were the last stand for liberty, but it balanced on our concealment lasting long enough. Long enough for what exactly? I don't honestly know. It's a strange reality. We live in the paradox of freedom with the caveat that we cannot leave. However, we knew of no other place to go, and returning to what we left was untenable.

That night, I had a vivid dream of the meteorite painting coming to life.

My grandad and I were standing on a ledge. Across a small valley, we watched the powerful release of energy as a meteorite ripped across the mountainside. And yet I felt no fear. We were somehow insulated from harm. He was saying something, but the noise of the impact drowned out his words. I woke up trying to make sense of it.

I knew intense, vivid dreams like this were a strange combination of memories and lessons GD taught me. They meant something important, and I lay awake in the darkness trying to understand his message. Without warning, I heard his voice as clearly as if he were there with me. "It's time," he said. That might seem like a cryptic message to many, but I knew exactly what it meant. It was time to spill my findings, time to collaborate, time to find this place, this Cali Bantu.

The fullness of morning took forever to arrive. I watched every minute of the next two hours tick by, waiting for an appropriate time to get up and not alarm my mom. I had to think out my strategy, present my information logically, and hold back just enough so that I couldn't be left out of the search. Gray may be mad. I was researching on my own without including them, but I had a beef to hash out with him too. And I was ready.

I sat with my family trying to have a relaxed breakfast. My parents could tell my mind was occupied, but they dismissed it because I was that kind of kid. They had no idea what I was involved in, no idea who I was. I told them I needed to talk with Gray, and they didn't even ask why. They trusted Gray, and they should. But it disappointed me that they didn't even ask me what it was about. They just turned over their parental rights to him, confirming that me and my pursuits scared them.

I should be happy because I would have needed to lie to them, or at the least, tell a half-truth. They took Libby home with them, leaving me alone at the table. I hadn't yet secured a meeting with Gray, but I was sure he'd answer the message I was about to send.

My note said simply, "It is imperative we meet!" I had never said or sent a message with urgency before, and it only took three minutes for him to reply. He asked what it was about, and I responded simply, "GD". He said he was bringing around a cart to pick me up. He was in front of the diner in under five minutes.

"We can't talk in this open cart," I said. "Can we go to the Security Building or something?"

He considered me for a second. "I'll ask Bannon, Rand, and Haru to join us."

"Not yet," I said.

He turned and focused on the street, and I felt the cart speed up. He settled me in the security briefing room and closed the door. While he filled a pitcher with water and grabbed a couple of glasses, I pulled out the rumpled papers of tri-column notes from my pocket. I could feel the childish action had him thinking this was not as critical as I had inferred. He'd learn soon enough that this information was so critical, it couldn't be trusted to a tablet.

"So, Connor, what's up?" he said, standing at the head of the table while pouring us each a glass of water.

"I know where it is, O.G. Or, at least, I know how to find it."

"Find what?" he asked casually, but I could tell I had his attention.

"I know where Cali Bantu is." I dropped it hard, wanting to see his mood flip.

He sank into his chair and threw out his hands. "For crap's sake, Connor. Where did you hear about that? Do you even know what *it* is?"

"When I was tutoring Sandra, I learned lip reading, so I could teach it to her. I thought it would help her talk to others more than sign language, which only a handful of people knew. She got her hearing back before she had the skill down, but I am pretty good at it. I saw Rand say it when I was tying Libby up that day I joined you guys for lunch. And yes, I inferred *it* was a place where a weapon or a cache of weapons is stored," I smiled.

"Of course you did. Lip reading," he said under his breath with exasperation. "I could go into the morality of eavesdropping, but let's skip the lecture for now. Tell me what you think you know."

I explained how the desk scroll and the symbols on the base of Vadina generated a map of a cave. I shared that Nitu Cabal meant beautiful rebellion, and it was easy to see they used the same letters in Cali Bantu. I explained there was a message under GD's desk that I needed Rand's help with. I told him about everything except the painting. I panicked at the thought of giving away everything GD entrusted to me. They might confiscate it, and I'd never see any of it again. It was a lie of omission, but a lie just the same because I knew it was a critical piece of the puzzle. Holding it back was the same as saying it didn't exist. But I needed a card to play in case they tried to cut me out. I justified it because I knew the mission would fail without GD's knowledge, the knowledge he entrusted to me.

"With that, the sketchbook, the sword scroll, and all the decoding techniques he shared with me, I think we can find the cave called Cali Bantu."

Gray just sat there. He looked at me like I was a conundrum, and I guess I was. He held his head up with his fingers on his forehead and his thumb on his cheek. He stayed that way for a long pause before he spoke.

"Well, I always knew you were smart. I think we'll take it from here though."

"I think not," I said. "I know for a fact that these revelations are new to you. I was designed to remember and trained to read these clues. You need me, and you know it." I was right. It was all being taken.

"Connor, you're eleven. These discoveries, if true, are dangerous."

"I'll be twelve soon. In the world I was raised in, I would be an apprentice worker and not considered a child anymore. I just moved to the high school. Though I'm the youngest kid there, all my studies are at the college level.

"I can solve these clues. My grandad planted the formulas and techniques in my head to decode the clues he left in this town. I'm sure he thought he would be here himself, but I was his contingency plan. I was born to take on this mission. It's my destiny. You can't deny it, and you can't prevent me from fulfilling it."

He sighed and leaned back in his chair. He squeezed his head between his elbows and slowly blew out a full breath. "Look," he said flopping his arms on the chair rests, "I can't believe I'm having this discussion with a kid, but regardless, I can't make any decisions on my own, and I need Rand to verify what you've found. We'll start there. I'm going to call them here," he said while reaching for the phone.

"Wait," I said. "I have one more thing to discuss with you." He looked apprehensive, and I felt his intimidating stare attempting to pin me down. He was a very powerful man, but I had very powerful information, so he listened. "What happened to Zoey's Aunt Merita?"

Gray cringed and leaned forward. "Zoey shouldn't have told you about that."

"She was scared and alone. She needed to trust someone, and she trusted me. I didn't ask her even though I was curious about it. It just spilled out of her when we went to visit the wall. Don't punish her. She's just a little kid."

"Hmm," he chuckled and gave me a sarcastic look. "Being eleven yourself, I don't think you're in the position to be giving orders."

"What did you do with her aunt?" I asked, knowing he wouldn't tell me, but maybe I could read a tell in his reaction.

He sat poker-faced and answered simply, "We put her in custody."

"Here?"

"I can't tell you that."

"Why did she try to run away with Zoey? Was she going to hurt her?"

"I can't tell you that either."

"I learned at school that residents get a trial before they can be punished."

"Her crime and culpability were discussed at length. But in the end, she wasn't a resident. She was an imposter, an infiltrator, and an addict. The leaders decide what to do with invading combatants, not the people." I could see he was going to shut me down. "Connor, I don't like where this conversation is going. Remember what I said about boundaries? You've just hit one."

"Was it kept from the town because she knew some secret? I know secrets. Secrets, I'm pretty sure you can't afford to let come out at a trial. Could I disappear if I got in trouble?"

He rolled his eyes and let out a long breath. "I see where you are going. Yes, she did have intelligence that could hurt this town severely. But everyone here has at least one secret, this town. No one can leave because sharing the existence of this place could destroy us and our hope for a better world outside too.

"When you were on the outside, you did everything in your power to protect your family and your grandad's secrets. Merita was an addict. All she cared about was her next buzz. She murdered her twin sister to get her next fix. If she had made it outside, she admitted that she planned to sell those secrets, and probably Zoey too. Did she understand what she was doing? Maybe, but the drugs made her not care.

"As the head defender of this town, it is my sworn duty to keep the people safe and this town secure from harm, and that includes you. I wish I could prevent you from digging into things, but you are driven to seek out answers to the mysteries you uncover. Some of these secrets put you and everyone else in danger." He was making his case to exclude me from the rest of the investigation and the expedition.

"But there is a big difference between you and her," he continued. "I know you would never do anything to hurt this town or its people. Countless times you've been allowed to leave a meeting knowing very sensitive information with no more than your promise not to tell."

"Yes," I agreed. They had demonstrated their trust in me. "I believe this is a virtuous place with moral intentions. I believe the people running it are honorable, but if they don't follow their own rules, I don't understand what that means. I can't be sure what could become of me."

"Connor, I promise you the people of this town and their leaders *are* good. We are so blessed. We have an incredible home with baseball, activities, festivals, and good food. We are secure in nice homes, and we wake up to beautiful renditions of the seasons and the passage of a day. People can pursue jobs they want, they are cared for, clothed, and educated. We have friendships and activities we never imagined in the Corporate world, but the ugly reality is, we are at war.

"A war we have left to those outside to fight until we are ready. The end goal of this whole project is to provide a reason to fight while we find the means to win. Everything about this place is to show people what is attainable for all, and that it's worth preserving. They need to understand and pass it down. They need to believe in the democratic system so fully that the only conclusion is everyone who wants it, deserves it. It's the duty of every *adult* to insure it." It did not escape my attention that he emphasized the word adult. "But we aren't ready yet. However, if your information proves true, it does bring us a lot closer."

"You don't ever have to worry about me telling anyone. I would never jeopardize this place."

"You have proven you can do that. How you managed that kind of discipline at your young age, I don't know. I believe that you would never want to, but horrible things you can't even imagine could be used to compel you. I know you are willing to make sacrifices to protect this town and its citizens, but it's not your job to protect us. It is *my job* to protect *you*," he said, pointing at me.

"Protecting me by leaving me out of the search may cause you to lose everything. You can protect me and everyone else by not excluding me. You need me to help you, and I'm supposed to do this, no matter what age I am. And I want to."

"I don't know what you think you are volunteering for, but I'm calling your parents and letting them know you will be here for a bit longer. Then I'm going to call Bannon, Rand, and Haru. Got it?"

"Yes," I said.

Our meeting ended with him making the calls he indicated. There was nothing to do but wait awkwardly in the hard silence for the next round and busy ourselves with empty tasks.

The clock said 9:13 when he called. Six minutes ticked by before they arrived. It was the longest six minutes I had ever lived through. One by one the three men filed in with attentive and concerned expressions. None of them spoke when they saw Gray's mood. They tensely took their seats quietly despite a multitude of unspoken questions.

Each one pulled out their pocket tablets and placed them on the table in a choreographed motion. It was Mr. Vogel who finally stirred the thick uneasiness.

"So, what's going on?" he asked with easy confidence. The irony of it caught me off guard. It was such a simple and casual inquiry for such a serious gathering. It was all so intense, making me press my lips together to suppress a laugh.

"He thinks he found Cali Bantu," Gray said, knowing shock would be the reaction. I had done that same thing to him, and he was passing it on. This was almost fun.

"Does it ever occur to any of you to introduce your subject without stunning your audience like they're your prey?" Haru was rolling his eyes.

"When the subject is as important as this, I hate dancing around the point," quipped Gray.

"Though your opening surprised me, the inevitability of the event did not. We all knew Connor would keep searching for answers to his grandad's legacy. Just as we all knew, the clues were all around us in this town."

"Well, I'm eager to hear what he's found," said Rand with unbridled excitement.

Mr. V. sat quietly observing the banter, and I waited for permission to speak.

"Normally, Connor, we would be required to have your parents present, but this subject is entirely too sensitive. Why don't you tell us in your own words what you have discovered," Mr. V. said, causing all eyes to turn toward me in robotic unison.

I explained to them what I had just shared with Gray. They didn't interrupt. They just took notes on their tablets. When I finished, all eyes were burning for permission to pummel me with questions.

Bannon turned to me. "Before we start hurling queries at you," he said and then faced the group. "Let's generate an agenda. We'll bring up these items and clues one by one. Everyone will get a turn to ask about them, and at the end, there will be another chance to revisit them. One more thing: this meeting will not last more than ninety minutes."

It was a comfort to know some form of order would be imposed on the anxious alphas sitting around the table waiting to pounce. The meeting ended on time with the initial plan of Rand investigating the desk. No one, especially me, wanted to alarm my parents that I was part of another risky venture. At some point, my parents would need to be informed, and I wondered if they would just hand me over to the fray. I wanted them to let me go, but I wanted them to care that I was going. Well, *if* I were going.

Rand sent a harmless virus to disrupt our home screen, so he would be summoned to our house when we were all at work and school. I wasn't happy he would reveal the message without me, but I had to accept that I wasn't working solo anymore. I was part of a team, but instead of playing for the public with balls and scores, this team was playing for keeps, cloak-and-dagger style. It was dangerous and exciting.

CHAPTER 19

The Security Building wasn't far from my house, and I needed to walk off the energy surging through me. They listened to me, included me, and together we made logical decisions. One of them was that my IS time would be replaced by what we were calling private lessons with Rand, but I would still participate in a couple of activities at school each week.

It was believable because my current lessons included difficult concepts to learn independently. It was another lie, a white lie. I *would* be working with him, and we *would* be engaging in scientific research and advanced logical studies, but it would be solely dedicated to a top-secret and dangerous assignment.

I thought about the painting I had held back from them. I knew it was critical to the whole picture because GD said so. Yet, it seemed odd that it fell into my lap so easily. It wasn't GD's nature to provide an answer to something as significant as Cali Bantu without a path of decoding to go through. The only thing that made it plausible was that no one but me would know it was his; however, it did infer that finding it would be difficult.

I had no idea where the mountain was located, and evidently, its appearance had been altered by the impact. It may require extended traveling to find it. We had other clues to weed through to shorten that journey. I couldn't give up the painting yet. Before I pulled it out, we needed to narrow down what mountain range it belonged to. I believed the clues from the castle, the desk, and the sketchbook would accomplish this better than the painting.

I was drawn out of my introspection by a group of people walking with handmade signs resting on their shoulders. I was too far away to read them, but they turned down the central corridor, no doubt to Town Hall. I decided to make a detour to check out the event.

As I approached the edge of the corridor, I saw at least a dozen more people in front of Town Hall. They were divided into two sections shouting their opposing arguments. On one side, the signs read, *Adulthood Now, Voting Rights Now,* and *Soldiers or Children; we can't be both.* The other side included messages like *Protect Parental Rights, Don't Break-up Families,* and, *Children shouldn't be Soldiers.*

The proposal was about lowering the age of consent from twenty-one to nineteen. It had as much support as it had opposition. I was witnessing a protest. I had never seen one outside of historical videos. I wondered how the town leaders would react.

I was shocked by the defiant display, but I was intrigued too. Several passers-by accused the rabble-rousers of acting unappreciatively, but it was evidence that the citizens were involved and interested in their government. It was proof that they believed in their right to voice concerns. The young men and women wanting their adult status had a valid point. This age group was too old to be minors still under parental control when many worked adult jobs. It was almost lunchtime, and I needed to get to the high school for a debate. Reluctantly, I left the chanting crowd, hoping to hear more details on the news tonight.

After school, I helped at Wally's for a couple of hours and walked home. "Hi," I yelled as Libby greeted me at the door.

"Come see this," my mom said. "Someone new is joining our town. Our screen is down, so we'll have to watch it on our tablets." I snickered, a bit surprised that Rand had already made his move.

"We were just watching the news of a Fringer girl that one of the mission teams brought back with them. She is going to join our town. The reporter was telling us what he learned about Fringers, and it suddenly just shut off," my mom sounded alarmed, and she was already on her tablet calling up the missed report.

I understood her concern. She was worried about having a Fringer in our town. We were taught they were dangerous criminal tribes of people who lived in the wilderness just outside of our territories. They were blamed for kidnappings, theft, and murders, but those accounts had come from the Corporates. It was clear the information they told us was layered with ulterior motives.

Though I was suspicious of the Fringers, there was no doubt the Corporates were oppressive and dishonest. I have since learned that *everything* they told us was to sustain their status quo of control. I grabbed my tablet and turned to the news. I chose the one titled *Newcomer* and listened to the story of a girl and her mother kidnapped by Drangers. They murdered her mother, and the girl was on her way to an abusive life in Pueblo when Jax and Axle rescued her. She had a serious injury, so they brought her to New Haven. It explained why Axle and Jax required a stint in quarantine. I hoped they were getting along.

The story went on to dispel the rumors about Fringers. They were mostly peaceful nomadic tribes who had escaped the confines of the Corporate territories. They had hard lives in the wilderness, in makeshift tents with few amenities. I thought about that. Though it would have been a difficult way to live, they were free to make their own choices. I can see why we were conditioned to fear them.

Her name was Aniya, and she was being treated in the quarantine area of the hospital for a severely broken leg and malnutrition. She was to be released in five days, but we could send her a welcome message and communicate with her on a chatline. We discussed it briefly as a family, and we decided to each write her a short message of welcome.

Next, we all clicked on *Protest at Town Hall*. The couple dozen people I saw at lunchtime had grown to at least forty or fifty. Though the biggest group was the college crowd, the parents had made their presence known too. The report showed Officer Gray addressing them.

"We hear both sides," he said. "And just to be clear, everyone here between nineteen and twenty-one signed a paper agreeing to the existing laws." Cheers and jeers rang from the parent crowd. "BUT," his voice boomed, "our goal was to secure your consent to confinement in New Haven, not in your parents' houses." Shouts came from the youth after that statement.

He regained their attention and continued. "Send your concerns to your representatives. Within the week we will call an emergency session to discuss housing and voting rights and address your concerns."

Undistinguishable comments were shouted at him, but he gestured for quiet, and once again they listened. "Nothing will be decided here tonight. The legislature needs time to discuss and write a bill before it can be presented to you. Go home. You will hear the proposal very soon, and then you can contact your representatives with your concerns."

Most of the crowd began filing off, but stragglers were still loitering when the news crew ended the bulletin.

"That was so cool," I said with enthusiasm.

"Are they going to get rounded up, Dad?" asked Mesh, remembering the way dissenters used to be dealt with.

"No," my dad said. "I think the town leaders will do what Officer Gray said they would. They will have an orderly conversation and base their decision on New Haven's Constitution and the will of the people." I noticed he was already on the repair request page submitting our faulty screen.

"Exactly," I agreed, "we got to see democracy in action. It makes me love this place more!" *Thanks, GD.*

New spring buds appeared on the bare trees, and containers of bushes were being replaced by flower pots that looked ready to bloom. My mom had joined the decorative plant brigade, which traded and enhanced the foliage around the town to fit the seasons. It was an easy, once-a-week duty that could be accomplished at the volunteers' leisure. She was also on the Independence Day committee. The anniversary of the town closing its access doors was September 15. A large celebration was being planned at Treagan Park. Although there was hope it could be held outside, the weather in September made it unlikely.

I have been meeting with Rand in his office for several weeks now. His office was an interesting space of contrasts. On one side sat his desk, which was as neat as can be. His computer and office supplies sat meticulously positioned on a dust and stain-free desk. Its only decoration was a Newton's cradle. I set them in motion, transfixed by the uniform way the swinging balls ticked off time. He looked irritated that I had disrupted his orderly area but refrained from saying so.

I gestured to the other side of his office in my defense. It looked like a storm had just blown through. Papers, books, and clipboards covered every available space. An unwashed coffee cup with rumpled candy wrappers sat in a holder on the drafting board while another teetered on his folder pile. He had a bookshelf, but it held more action figures than books. He said that sometimes he needed a clean space to work and other times the clutter inspired him.

He went to our house and tested a corner of the message. After evaluating its chemical makeup, he concluded a mild vinegar would cause the paint to turn dark and make it visible, but only temporarily. There were two messages. One was written in Egyptian hieroglyphs, and the second was written in code. Translating the hieroglyphs was straightforward, but what they said wasn't. It had nothing to do with the information we had deciphered so far. The translated hieroglyphs read:

Egyptian mountains test the will of man against time.

It sounded like a poetic platitude, which allowed one to apply any meaning they wanted to it. The next section had actual clues and made more sense. It read:

Dwelling in the darkest fears,
Where her soldiers bravely lay,
The Sanguine Blade frees the spears,
To stand against the fray.

"What's a Sanguine Blade? Is it a knife or a sword?" asked Rand.

I shrugged my shoulders. "It's capitalized, so it's a specific one. The word sanguine means blood, so it could be a weapon used in battle. Or it could be a murder weapon that would prove someone's guilt. I can't imagine uncovering a murderer would change anything. I'm guessing it's the blade the castle scroll referred to. 'Dwelling' and 'darkest' sound like descriptions of a cave, so at least that's related to what we have so far."

"I think you're right about the scroll reference. I'm running a computer search on every keyword I can think of," he said, flowing over the keyboard with impressive finesse.

I was rubbing my forehead hoping to massage out an answer. "Maybe we're overthinking it. We are trying to force this piece into our current narrative. We need to let it find its rightful place. Let's look at this message by itself as if it were the first one."

Rand stopped and listened to me as his computer piled thousands of files on his screen.

"Okay, GD used to say, start with the simple facts. It's written in Egyptian hieroglyphs, so unlike letters, we can't scramble the symbols, but we can look for clues in the translation. It says, 'Egyptian mountains test the will of man against time'.

"Well, we can guess that 'Egyptian mountains' refers to pyramids, but I don't know of any pyramids near here," Rand said. "Logic dictates this cave is close enough for us to access without traipsing through other territories or traveling to other continents." He paused, thinking deeply while staring at a star chart on his wall. It was on the messy side of his office, and I assumed he was using it for inspiration.

"Egyptians are known for building the pyramids, which are riddled with tunnels where they kept treasures," I added.

"Maybe one of those treasures is the Sanguine Blade. Maybe it's a key to an armory. How will we locate it? Is it an actual blade, or something shaped like one?" Rand was looking at me, but I was stumped by this clue. GD never said anything about the Sanguine Blade. It was obvious I was getting into the deep recesses of his most dangerous secrets.

Rand cleared his piles of files and began tapping on his keyboard at light speed as if the milliseconds it would take to do so calmly would matter. "How about a mountain peak named Pyramid?" Rand said, ushering me over to look at various views of a peak in the Elk Mountain Range it was part of.

"Wow, if you were to add a huge meteorite scar across that view," I said, pointing to the one that displayed a close-up of the western view of the peak, "it would look like the landscape my grandad painted."

"The what?" Rand said, looking over his glasses with exasperation.

"It's something I didn't include on my list. It kind of slipped my mind," I lied. I had been worrying about it, and I wasn't sure which I regretted more, hiding it then or revealing it now.

"Really? It just slipped your eidetic mind?"

"I'm sorry. I shouldn't have held it back. I guess I wanted to think about it for a while longer on my own. Alex just pulled it out of storage. It's in the *Meteorite Geological Wonders* exhibit. When I saw it, I immediately flashed back to my memory of it. GD told me it was important, and I didn't see it again until a week ago. He signed it A.T.," I said with a smile, hoping he'd enjoy the irony and leap into an explanation of A.L.E.C.T. and stop being disappointed in me.

"Of course he did," and he relaxed his posture some. "A.L.E.C.T. or Alec T. is an acronym for the undercover group that conceived, created, and constructed this city," Rand disclosed. "It stands for Americans for Liberty, Ethics, Citizens, and Truth." That worked. I chuckled inside at his predictability.

"Yeah, I figured it was something like that when I was told it was a fake authorization name used for final approvals. It was too close to the word 'elect' to be a coincidence. I'm sorry. I should have told you about the painting. It wasn't easy coming here knowing I was giving up every important clue that GD put in my care," I said, flattening my palm against my chest for emphasis. "I didn't know you guys would include me, but you did, and I should have said something then. I was so focused on the desk, I told myself I'd tell you later. The painting is the last piece I know of. I promise."

"I get it, dude," he said with a sigh. "We needed to focus on those other clues first. It's possible we might have charged in without being as prepared as we are now. So, moving on, we know around where the cave is, but it's a big area. We need to narrow it down. We could spend years looking for a hidden entrance."

"Let's go through GD's sketchbook. He has tons of crazy entries. Maybe one has coordinates or something."

"And we still haven't deciphered the numbers on the sword scroll," he answered. "I'll go get both from the safe. I'm also going to ask Bannon if we can't requisition that painting. Can you stay through dinner? His notes are like a coded letter to you personally. I could use your help."

"I'll ask my parents. What shall I say we're working on that requires me to stay?"

"Well. I've been asked to set up the logistics for the Emerging-Age bill and the housing it would require. I'm supposed to present it tomorrow. I'm already done, but ..." he trailed off, not wanting to say I should lie, but at the same time providing me with perfectly plausible material. I was thick in the lying business, and it made me feel sleazy every time I did it, but it was becoming a go-to habit whenever the information was difficult. I dreaded the day it became easy.

Someday it would all come out. I wondered if anyone would believe what I said after that. I spent my whole life telling them what I thought they should know, justifying my lies for their protection. Yet, if people knew the truth about what I was working on, it would terrify them. They might try to stop us, and that terrified me.

We had dinner delivered and worked until eight. We gathered over thirty entries from GD's book, and Rand said he would run them through some combinations and permutations. Hopefully, it would pinpoint a coordinate in the Elk Mountains within the vicinity of Pyramid Peak.

CHAPTER 20

The Independence Day celebration was held inside, though we had blue skies outside. We knew that because a new channel called *Skyview* displayed a slide show of pictures from the outside cameras. I tried not to be paranoid, but if the weather wasn't the reason, then what was?

Activities were held at both Brad Anderson Park and Treagan Park. Patriotic music filled the air, and flying vehicles called fighter jets performed crazy stunts and zoomed across the ceiling. GD told me that many different kinds of aircraft used to fly over cities often to protect their nations as well as carry people to faraway lands.

My friends and I enjoyed the huge inflated slide that splashed into a shallow pool. It blocked the street section at Treagan almost as much as the lines to enjoy it did. We tried another ride that spun us around in giant chairs. I spent four of my credits earmarked for a scooter on fun and sweets. I had saved up eighteen credits, and now I was down to fourteen. The fun was worth it, but my belly was churning from eating junk food and dizzying rides. I felt like lying down, but I wanted to see the 9:30 fireworks show advertised on the Independence Day agenda.

By 9:25, the lights illuminating the festival had fully faded, leaving only low walking lights. Everyone's attention was on our tunnel skies. Suddenly, bursting lights cascaded across the ceiling accompanied by crackling pops. The colors were vibrant, and each flare streaked across the sky like shooting stars. The display crescendoed until a dazzling finale exploded across the curved tunnel ceiling. I was exhausted by the time I got to bed, but it was worth it. I fell asleep thinking of the world we had created in this vulnerable bubble, and how I would do everything in my power to keep it safe.

The vote on the Emerging-Age bill was passed. Like most decisions made in a free society, it was a compromise. The residents, aged nineteen to twenty-one, could elect one representative from their age group to engage in discussions and vote at the congressional sessions. This would provide them with official representation for their unique concerns.

They were also allowed to apply for residency in the dorms. Plans to increase dorm space, create group housing, and build a Defender bunkhouse were already in progress. Though there were over two dozen vacant houses ready for the town's growing inhabitants, population control remained a critical issue.

Another construction project was to turn a large storage area across from the church into a club for seventeen to twenty-year-olds. Only non-alcoholic beverages would be served since the drinking age remained a twenty-one and over law. A naming contest was held among the intended patrons, and the winner was Derechos. A derecho is a fierce, windy storm, and it described this group's energy well.

I thought about the high-level tasks I was working on and the irony of being cleared for such critical duties but not considered mature enough for any of these privileges. Though I would like to vote, I wasn't interested in going to a hang-out where Sandra might be.

I smiled, thinking about Haru handing out invitations to church activities as the patrons stood in line to gain access to the club. No doubt he'd get a bigger teenage crowd for activities on the days the Derecho was closed. Although another round of parent protests erupted, the number of participants had dwindled to a small handful who finally accepted the decision.

It was early October, meaning spring was blooming around the town. A new celebration was being launched called Halloween. It was an old holiday jumbled with bits and pieces from multiple religions. The activities included dressing in costumes, taking on character roles, and participating in a parade. There was talk of a contest, but I was unaware what it entailed. We would be able to pick our character from the many racks of costumes that were saved from theaters before they were seized, closed, or burned.

Both of the schools gave the same assignment to all their students. Choose three characters we wished to portray and why. Rand gave me the same eye-rolling assignment. We were in the final stage of our findings, and this task paled in comparison. But I agreed; it maintained our facade.

For my first costume choice, I selected an archeologist. The other two choices were mountain climber and professional baseball player. It gave me a reason to study people who search for lost artifacts and who go on wilderness adventures. The knowledge I gathered from researching those two occupations could come in handy. My friends questioned me about my lack of enthusiasm for the event. I tried to act excited about it, but I wasn't. I was preoccupied, and I couldn't tell them why.

Rand and I had our own exciting news. We had worked into the evening, and we believed we had found the side of the mountain with the entrance to the cave of Cali Bantu. The next afternoon, we had an appointment to give our report. I tossed and turned that night between the pure joy that we found it to absolute fear I wouldn't be allowed to go. I knew with complete certainty the destination would be riddled with traps and locks. The kind I've been trained to open. I had to go.

For the rest of the town, it was a typical Wednesday, but not for Rand and me. This afternoon, we would present our exciting news. While I anticipated our culminating meeting, Hayden messaged me that this weekend we'd be allowed to try on costumes. I wished I could tell him that I wasn't in school anymore, but I lied and said I had a project to present, and I'd contact him later. Lie, lie, lie, it was unbearable.

After finalizing our meeting and helping Dewy, I headed to the Town Hall. I love to walk in the safety of our town as I contemplate the good fortune of life here and compare it to my old life. It helped me to justify my dishonest behavior as a noble sacrifice. We wouldn't be here if secrets weren't kept and lies were exposed. I thought about how different it was to be a student instead of a laborer. I had recently turned twelve, so outside I would have been working as an apprentice with no school, no sports, just work. I was happy my talents were being utilized to restore and maintain freedom instead of being wasted on backroom lessons, but I was still hiding behind a false persona.

I had heard that the Upper kids, who were allowed to go to school, hated it. I assumed their schools weren't like ours. Or maybe they just hadn't experienced the alternative of day after day of back-breaking labor and the ache of persistent hunger. Even though school is hard and frustrating at times, I love those moments when the fog clears and a concept clicks into place.

School is still work, but it is all about moving toward a future *I* want. My days used to be full of hard work, and though it helped my family, it was never going to get me anywhere I wanted to be. I hope the kids growing up with freedom don't come to hate school because they didn't learn how hard life is without the choices education provides.

All of a sudden, I was shocked out of my introspection by the repeating wail of a lockdown alarm. The lights dimmed, and a pulsing red hue lit up the ceiling where our peaceful sky had been. I froze in place. I knew the drill, but I was stunned by the reality. Maybe this was a surprise drill. Yeah, that's it. Having those would be smart.

"Please report to your Hostile Force stations. This is not a drill," said the robotic voice from the tunnel speakers. I froze in disbelief. The composed voice didn't fit the mood, but the blaring siren did. I hadn't moved yet, but it began to seep in that a real threat was imminent or actually happening. The message repeated itself before I moved from my frozen spot. Soon after that, the rain started falling. It seemed metaphorical, but I knew the automated system was running through its fire prevention protocol.

Panic swelled through my chest, and my heart was pounding a double time beat joining the pulsing lights and the raucous wah, wah sound of the alarm. I was alone. Libby was alone. I knew I was required to go to the library, but I ran home instead. *Please,* I prayed, *don't let us be too late to save this town.*

Libby greeted me at the door, bouncing around like a wild creature. She was happy to see me, but it did not dissuade her fear. Check my tablet, I thought. It opened up to a page that outlined the Hostile Force protocols.

In the event of a Hostile Force Lockdown, you will report to your assigned stations. Essential personnel will report to their workstation according to the schedule provided by their supervisors. Children will report to their homes or their schools according to each family's plan. Parents may pick up their children from schools or other places unless or until full restrictions are in place.

Secure all doors and windows and close all curtains. If you are not in your designated area, send a message and your picture to this number, 555. It will be available to all persons cleared to know.

Any children seen outside on their own should be brought inside your area and a message immediately sent to the number above with their name and picture.

If the tunnel is breached, further instructions will be provided. Turn to channel 911 for updates.

CHAPTER 21

W hile I was sending a message to report my whereabouts, the alarms stopped sounding. I went outside hoping the whole thing was resolved, or better yet a mistake. But the lights were still pulsing an eerie red glow on the ceiling and the puddled street. I quickly went back inside.

I got a message from my dad, saying he was picking up Mesh, and then he'd be home. My mom worked in Town Hall in the records department. My guess was she was busy dumping sensitive material. I sat for a few minutes, not wanting to hear what I already knew. Our world was ending. If we were found, we were done.

I felt riddled with guilt, and I just couldn't bear to turn on the news report. All this adult responsibility and I was folding like the notes in my pocket. *Shoot, I had dangerous information in my pocket.* I ripped it into tiny pieces and threw it in the compost toilet. Within minutes it would be unreadable.

I went to my room and stood by my shelf. I picked up New Haven's first game ball that was gifted to me for reviving baseball and starting the league. I looked at the picture of me, my friends, and Hannah taken at the final games just days before she died. The worry for Gray, Axle, and every Defender further took hold of my heart.

I should have worked harder on the clues instead of playing on teams and tutoring students. Instead, I kicked back and enjoyed my freedom and leisure time while the enemy plotted our downfall. Maybe I could have found Cali Bantu sooner, and then they wouldn't be attacking us. We would have brought the fight to them first. It occurred to me that my mind rant was premature. I didn't know what was actually happening. I assumed it was the Corporates, but maybe it was the Fringers. They would be easier to defeat, at least that's what I had been led to believe. My head spun. I didn't even know for sure what Cali Bantu was or what it contained, but I should. *GD, I've let you down. I'm so sorry.*

My father found me weeping softly in my room. Libby was sitting by my feet while I looked through my precious memories.

"Connor," he said anxiously, and he grabbed me in a hug like I had just been found wandering alone in the darkness. It was exactly how I felt.

"Dad, what does this all mean? Did we get a taste of paradise, so for the rest of our lives we can commiserate on bygone days and 'if onlys?' like GD, I said in my head. Maybe that misery will be shortened by our executions or endless torture. No, no, no, this can't be happening.

"Let's go downstairs and turn on the screen. We need to stay positive for Meska. She's scared too, but you know what she said to me? She said, 'But we've got this right, Dad?' Maybe she's right, Connor. Maybe it's not as bad as we think."

I followed him downstairs, and Libby followed me. Mesh was sitting alone, staring at the now working screen. "What does it say, Dad?" she asked. Her innocence glowed like an aura.

Vague answers came on a pale grey background with a bulleted message in black print. My dad read the screen out loud.

- *Today, armed Dranger and Neighwah soldiers were seen approaching the tunnel on both sides.*

- *Our Defenders are currently engaging the enemy.*

- *We believe this is only a reconnaissance mission.*

- *Please remain at your current locations until further notice.*

- *Use your emergency supplies sensibly.*

- *You may watch downloaded movies on low volume. (5 or less)*

- *Keep your screen active until further notice, so you can receive new information.*

It was absurdly calm and bleakly devoid of the details we craved. I immediately thought of all the lies I was involved with, and I knew this explanation was woefully unreliable. I couldn't help at the command station, but right now was about protecting my family. But how? We had no weapons and no way to contact our mom, our neighbors, or our friends on our tablets. The only message we could send was to the 555 designation if we had something to report. Surely hiding wasn't our only plan. The adults must know more about how to defend New Haven.

My dad decided to turn on a downloaded movie, but what we wanted to watch was what was going on outside. Libby climbed onto the couch where she wasn't allowed, but today I welcomed her onto my lap. My dad loaded a cartoon movie about a mermaid that Zoey had been asking to watch. My mind was exploding. I couldn't just sit here and do nothing.

I left Libby cuddled on the couch in Meshka's arms, and I went up to my room. I tried to watch a basketball game on my tablet, but it felt wrong. How could I enjoy any form of entertainment while our town was under siege and our Defenders were locked in battle?

I looked at the clock, and only sixteen minutes had passed since the alarm first sounded. Impossible! It felt like time was being altered. Each moment was so heavy, it struggled to move to the next. The most unnerving thing of all was the absence of battle sounds. A war was going on, and my friends were fighting it, maybe to the death. Outside, battle cries were snarled among booming guns, and exploding ordinances while we were drowning in the maddening silence. Did I want to hear it? No... well, maybe because at least it would make sense, more sense than watching a movie.

I got on my knees and prayed. I prayed for my mom, whom I assumed was okay because my dad said he had heard from her. I prayed for the Defenders. I prayed for the town. I prayed for my dad, Meshka, and all my friends. And I prayed for me. I prayed to be forgiven.

I settled on my bed and opened my tablet. All my tablet notes were erased, one more signal of how serious the danger was. I hoped it was not gone forever. Then I thought of all the information that was most likely being dumped. How would we ever reclaim it?

I thought of the drawings of the mountain I had hidden in my room, and I wondered what I should do with them. I retrieved them, tore them into pieces, and went downstairs to stuff them in the compost toilet. I could redraw and write what I had discovered. Still, it would take time. Time we did not have.

The wait was tormenting my thread-bare nerves. I cried. I punched my pillow, and I cried some more. I wanted to help, to grab a gun and go out fighting. It wasn't fair. We couldn't lose this battle. We couldn't lose this place. I paced my room feeling vulnerable and anxious. I crumpled, weeping and curled on the floor. *GD please, please send me a sign. Tell me what to do.*

I got up. All my wailing would do no good. I walked to the baseball poster that hung on my wall and ran my fingers over the silky championship baseball ribbon pinned to it. I thought of all the rooms and all the things that reflected the interests, dreams, and hopes of our town.

We had come so far. We now know what it means to be free, to trust, and to believe in something we were a part of as opposed to owned by. I stopped my pacing. "I won't let it go," I growled out loud. If I were still breathing, there was still a way to fight for what I believed in. This is a time for action, not reaction.

All this time, I had resented being treated like a child, but I am a child. And in a crisis, like a child, I was drowning in inexperience and counting on childish wishes and futile bargaining. It was then I remembered something

GD's told me. *It is pointless to pout over the trials of hindsight. Disappointment is a call to action.* He was right, as usual. I am more than a child. I am a highly trained researcher. I am a Highmind created to save democracy. The cause needs me now more than ever. It was time to act, and I was ready. We *will* find Cali Bantu, and we *will* be victorious.

I stood at the balcony window and peeked outside. Nothing stirred but the menacing red strobing lights. No Defenders patrolled the streets, so the threat was contained outside. They undoubtedly were positioned at the tunnel entrances. Looking at my watch, twenty-five minutes had passed. Good grief, how could so much happen in such a small block of time? I had spent enough energy and time to climb a mountain. This wait for information was intolerable. I wanted to scream and not at volume five or less. Just then, my dad called me downstairs.

"Look," he said, "Haru is speaking. It interrupted Meshka's movie. Do you want to join us?"

I settled down on the big chair next to the couch. I trusted Haru. His calm voice and enduring faith were comforting. Not like all-is-well comforting, but it was a relief of sorts. As I listened, my stress level did drop, at least enough to sit still.

Twenty more minutes crawled by when the coveted message finally came. As before, it came in simple bulleted statements:

- *The battle is over.*

- *The enemy has retreated.*

- *An approaching storm should prevent any further attacks.*

- *You may now venture outside, but remain within your neighborhood block.*

- *Please avoid the* hospital, *where the staff is busy attending to the wounded.*

- *Any non-emergency medical needs should be addressed at the Rapid Aid Center.*

- *In one hour, a bus will begin delivering to-go meals.*

- *We will report the casualty list after we have confirmed our information and notified family members.*

Their messages weren't big on details, and questions ran like a grocery list through my mind. It confirmed that we had injured soldiers. But how many and who? How badly? Did anyone die? Did we win, or did they leave because of the storm? What happens when the storm is over? What happens now that we are discovered?

"Dad, can we send word to Mom now?" I asked.

"Yeah, I just sent her a message. I'm just waiting for her reply. I imagine she is neck-deep in protocols," he answered while watching his tablet like a pot set on the stove to boil.

Suddenly, the screens on all of our tablets lit up, and my mom was smiling back at us.

"Hi, I can't talk long, but I just wanted to touch base and let you know I'm fine. I monitored the resident reports, so I knew all of you made it home safely. You can message me if you need to, but I'm quite busy, so I may not get back to you. Take care, and I'll be home soon." Our display went back to the home screens.

I wanted desperately to contact Rand, Gray, and Axle. Was Dewy in the fight? He had only just recently healed enough to walk without his cane. The exasperating wait began all over again.

It was evening when the high school social studies teacher came on to give his report. He was the one who oversaw the news program delivered by the high school journalism students. He must have thought that the shocking nature of this report required his personal attention.

"Good evening, this is Marcus Miller with New Haven News.

I have decided to give this report myself. It will be brief but informative. Let me start by telling you that we won this battle. It was not the storm that drove the enemy away. We had an assist. An army of Fringers led by William of the Guard came to our aid. Without their help, you would be hearing a very different report tonight."

A picture came on the screen of a tall, muscular black man walking across the area within our western barrier. He wore archaic leather armor, which was splattered with blood. He sported a wound seeping from beneath a primitive cloth bandage tied around one of his large bare bicep. He looked like a brutish warrior from another time.

"His army attacked the enemy from behind as they made their way to our tunnel entrances. They fought relentlessly, with thin armor and obsolete weaponry. But with their help, we won this battle."

It did not escape my attention that it was the second time he had used the word battle. If he had said we had won the war, that would be a very different thing. A battle was an event in a war, so it insinuated the war was still active. This would not be the last incursion.

Several months ago, after the attack on our people at the Hold, the Guard stumbled upon the facility. We know they did not have anything to do with the attack because the Defenders leave no survivors. Finding it uninhabited, they moved in, and they have been living and training their army there. They have united many of the Fringer tribes, which has allowed them to build a strong army. Allying our people with them is our best hope of protecting our way of life.

And now for the more tragic news. We lost two of our Defenders, Parker McCallum and Gedediah Nelson. Our hearts go out to their friends as they had no family members in New Haven. Seventeen Defenders received medical attention for ambulatory wounds. Three Defenders were hospitalized, and one is in critical condition.

The Guard army lost ten soldiers; many are wounded, and one is in critical condition. We thank all the soldiers who defended our home. We grieve our losses and those of our new friends. Their service will be remembered and honored always, and we pray all the injured will heal fully. Goodwill messages may be sent to the 555 address.

In light of our discovery and the bravery of our Guard partners, talks are now underway to solidify an official alliance. Updates on the talks and the condition of our soldiers will be reported as we receive more information.

Thank you, this is New Haven News signing out.

CHAPTER 22

I was saddened to hear the Fringers lost so many of their Guard soldiers. They fought outside the barrier with meager armor and weapons. Their sacrifice weighed heavily on my conflicted trust. I was shocked to hear they controlled the Hold. We were told his people weren't involved in the incident that killed Hannah and injured Dewy. They say the enemy who ambushed our Defenders were Drangers, and all of them had been killed. But how did they know that for sure? What proof did they have? I was not ready to trust the Fringers.

I also wanted to know who our critically injured soldier was. Although every Defender had my heartfelt wishes for recovery, Axle, Gabe, Gray, and Dewy held a special place in my world, and I couldn't imagine losing any one of them. Well, actually, I could imagine it. I lived through it once, and I didn't care to add another name to my anguish.

I thought about this Fringer army. We had been re-educated regarding the Fringers when Aniya came to our town as a refugee. She worked with Billie at the ranch, and I met her once. She was tall, with green eyes and a halo of golden hair. She was stunningly beautiful, but that was why she was targeted.

She was quiet and shy with fearful undertones, like Zoey, like all of us were at first. We had the Hold training, which we went through as a community. She lived very differently. She belonged to a tribe of free individuals. She had also spent her whole life outside in the forest. I wondered how she would adjust to life in a tunnel. Like us, she had experienced horrible violence, but unlike us, she would have to manage those issues on her own as a foreigner.

I still had lingering doubts and fears about lawless rogue tribes that even the Corporates didn't mess with. Forming an alliance seemed logical on the surface, but it was premature. Why can't the discussion wait until we are resettled? Unless the reason is another attack is looming sooner than we have been led to believe.

So many thoughts were running through my head, but the big, puffy chair in our living room felt comfortable, and exhaustion overtook my curiosity. The next thing I knew, my dad was waking me up for dinner. Libby was snuggled on my lap. How quickly our rule of no dogs on the furniture had disintegrated after one evening's lapse. Meshka was on the couch stretching and yawing off the nap she also had awoken from.

"Come on, the dining bus is here. We need to get our to-go meals," my dad said as he stood by the door.

My sister wandered over to our dad while I went to the bathroom. Checking myself in the mirror, I splashed some water on my unruly waves and swept them in line with my fingers. I had recently got a haircut, but he left the top too long. I thought about getting my hat and decided against it. "Good enough," I muttered.

We decided to eat in the yard at the picnic table. We invited our two neighbors, Mel and Mandy, because their parents were at work. They happily joined us in line to get our to-go meals in hand. I hardly knew them, but I should have . I was assigned to the high school now, which might have remedied that if I actually attended. And though we've lived as neighbors for a year, I never paid much attention to them. But today, they looked different somehow.

Melody had on a tight pair of black pants and a loose tan T-shirt, and Amanda wore her jeans and a short pink sweater revealing occasional glimpses of her belly. Both girls had long, dark, shiny hair that flowed freely around their shoulders. I never noticed how beautiful my neighbors were until today. Maybe, like me, they had gotten older.

We stood quietly waiting for our boxed meals while observing a simmering crowd of adults talking near the bus.

"We have to do something," said an incensed neighbor. "We should have formed a bigger army."

"Yeah, instead of all these recreation facilities, we should have been making weapons," said another irate member of my housing section. We gathered our rations quickly and slipped behind the short fence of our yard to distance ourselves from the escalating conversations. We sat down at the picnic table in our shared yard while Libby waited by our feet for stray tidbits.

"Mr. Wayther, I get we won the battle, and it's sad Defenders got hurt and killed, but what is going on with us and the Fringers?" asked Mel, the ninth grader, as Mandy, the seventh grader, looked on with unsure eyes.

"Well, I think we are all waiting to hear the details of that, but they joined our fight, and as far as we know, they didn't have to. The report said we most likely would have lost if they didn't, and we would not be sitting at our homes having a meal right now. Those are the facts I got from the report. I believe they want something from us. My guess is it is the same thing we need from them, an alliance.

"Another fact is we have been discovered, and that was just the first battle. We cannot win a war against the Corporates by ourselves. Having joined us, they will be targeted and blamed along with us for retaliating against the regime. They must feel threatened by the Corporates too, or they wouldn't have joined our fight.

"It sounds like the Guard army is much larger than ours, and to win against the Neighwah and Drangers, they must be well trained and organized. With their numbers and our better weapons and armor, we are stronger together. The only thing left is to hammer out what that will look like."

"That sounds like a good thing, so why are people so mad?" said Mandy. I watched her slurping the Chinese noodles when one slapped her cheek. I laughed like it were funny, but it was adorable.

"I think they're scared," my dad said softly. "We have been told we shouldn't trust the Fringers our whole lives. It's hard to turn those beliefs off." We all paused silently, agreeing and concentrating on our meals.

Everything was at risk, and its value was incalculable. I thought of the answer to our dilemma gathering dust in a cave somewhere in the Elk Mountains. We had to secure it, whatever it was. And whatever it was, I hoped it was enough.

Mel and Mandy messaged their parents that they were hanging out at our house to play cards and watch a movie, and though we expected more news, no additional reports came that evening. I lay in bed awake until I heard my mom come home. I knew she was okay, but having her home allowed me to relax. I settled into a restless sleep, still reliving the day and imagining those to come.

We woke up the next morning to a news report that had been delivered early that morning. The high school teacher looked a bit disheveled in his brown tweed blazer sitting at a lightly cluttered desk, but he provided a straightforward report.

Marcus Miller here with the New *Haven News,*

The leaders worked through the night to negotiate an alliance with William of the Guard. That we needed to ally with each other was not in question. The purpose of the discussion was to decide the parameters.

An impending storm required the Guard to return to their base, so the lengthy process of gathering the citizens' opinions was not possible. The emergency protocol, initiated when the battle began, gave the New Haven Legislators the power to sign the agreement. The approved accord is summarized below.

The Alliance between New Haven and the Guard is as follows:

New Haven will provide the Guard with the following:

• continued access and residency to all four Hold buildings

• the agreed-upon resources

Both agreed to:

• continued peaceful interactions

• continued communication, negotiations, and full disclosure of further alliances

• reciprocal military assistance as required

We are fortunate to be a part of a powerful alliance that stands for free self-governance. A complete copy of the bill will be available on your tablets later today.

The dining halls, schools, and most municipalities will resume their regular schedules tomorrow. The recreation facilities manned by Defenders are closed until further notice.

This is New Haven News signing out.

It was just as my dad had predicted. The logic of it did not concern me, but our new partners did. I too, wasn't sold on the Guard army as our saviors, but I wasn't sure we had much of a choice.

We checked out the list, and my mom said we could spare those items, confirming she was keenly aware of our inventory. One thing was sure: if we didn't have help to defend this place, we wouldn't be able to keep them, anyway.

We went to breakfast, and Libby was happy to take a walk. When we arrived at the dining hall, something was off. The energy level was high, too high. The fear emanating from dining residents was palpable, and the frustration it caused was transforming the crowd. Angry rhetoric flowed from every table and spilled over to the next. Even Meshka could see it was turning into a problem.

"Are the soldiers going to round us all up, Daddy? Can we take our food and go home?" She may only be eight, but she was wise enough to read the crowd.

"That's a good idea, Meshy. Let's order our food to go." After we put in our orders, he told us to wait outside the fence with Libby.

Before we left, diners were standing up to announce their irritation. Like us, they were scared, but unlike us, they were not thinking through it. They were consumed by dark emotions and fanning the flames of fear and rage. We saw a bus full of Defenders heading to the diner as we walked back to our house. I was upset at the unfairness of them having to fight another battle with the very people they shielded during the first.

We sat down in front of our screen and watched the live video report of the angry mob yelling in front of Town Hall. Officer Gray walked out and jumped up on a garden box to get everyone's attention.

"Residents of New Haven, it is plain to see you love your town, and we acknowledge your valid concerns. A time and place will be arranged to hear your grievances. A news feed will be sent within two hours to explain the goal and schedule for the town forums.

Please make your way to your jobs, homes, or other lawful activities. I ask you to respect this request on behalf of our Defenders. They are weary from battle. We have lost two Defenders, and we have four more recovering. They are, they were, our friends, family, neighbors, and fellow citizens of New Haven. We all need to take a breath. Take a moment to slow down to grieve. It is the respectful thing to do for now."

He stopped and observed the crowd. Most people looked more compliant, and the tone was calmer. When a few agitators started ramping up, he addressed the crowd again.

"HOWEVER," he said with a commanding tone, *"not complying with these orders will result in your arrest, credit fines, and a disorderly conduct record."*

There was the murmur and occasional outbursts displayed by the still-charged crowd, but they dispersed themselves in various directions.

The leaders had been on duty for over a day. Gray looked weary. I doubted he had slept yet. At least I knew Gray wasn't one of the injured, but there were four soldiers with significant injuries, and we still didn't know their names. Family members had been notified, but the rest of us would have to wait. That meant my friends could be among the wounded.

I was angry for those having to remain on duty to respond to these additional issues. I wondered what Bannon thought of his residents continually rallying against his creation. No doubt the angry people were exhausted too. And what about Ari? She was days from having her baby. I'm sure she worried about what the future held.

After all, we had been given, it seemed ungrateful to question the motives of our leaders, especially Bannon. Even during this, their darkest hour, their dedication to their responsibilities was relentless.

I thought about GD's description of democracy. "Democracy is messy and full of dissenters, but they only annoy us when their opinions differ from ours. Good leaders encourage a constant mixing and grinding of ideas to keep government relevant and honest."

I would add exhausting to the description.

CHAPTER 23

I woke up late the next morning. My parents let me sleep in. I took a longer and hotter than usual shower. Normally, I took pride in my attention to the conservation of resources, but today I needed to melt into the comfort a hot shower could provide. Today was Thursday, and I was supposed to report to city hall and work with Rand, but I had no idea if I would be allowed to go there after yesterday's battle.

I took a leisurely walk to breakfast and ordered the biggest one offered. I was hungry because I hadn't eaten much yesterday. I headed to Town Hall believing we might be meeting. I hoped they would fill me in on the injured soldiers and maybe some other details too, like who this Fringer warrior was, and whether we should trust his army band.

I wondered if Rand had shared our information without me. I kept waiting for them to say it was time for adults to take it from here, and I should step down. When I walked in, the receptionist greeted me. I expected her to send me back to school, but she told me to go immediately to the conference room. I made my way up the stairs at a half run.

Opening the door, I saw Gray, Bannon, Haru, and Rand sitting at the table. I feared this event was the final straw that made them decide to carry on without me, but I sat down acting like they had been waiting instead. "Sorry, I would have come earlier, but I wasn't sure we were doing this," I explained, adding that I wasn't invited in my head.

"In fact, you're right on time. I was just about to send for you," Bannon responded. "Let's hear what you guys have so far."

"Can I ask some questions first?" He nodded for me to continue. "Who are the injured soldiers? Did we win the battle, or did the storm get too bad to continue? And why do we trust this William of the Guard and his Fringer army? Oh yeah, and how is Ari doing?"

"Wow, that's more than a few questions, but I can answer all of them. All the injured soldiers are going to make full recoveries, including Axle, who was the most critically injured." I was alarmed and relieved in the same instant. He continued. "With the Guard's help, we defeated the Corporate soldiers. The storm was hours away before they retreated, but it prevented them from sending reinforcements.

"As far as trusting them, I think Gray put it best when he spoke to the legislators last night. He said everything they asked for, they either already had possession of or could have taken from us in our weakened state. We need them at least as much as they need us. And Ari had a baby boy last night, Sebastian Tomas, and both are well."

"So, you believe they will send reinforcements when the storm ends."

"We are making arrangements to deter that. But now, I want to hear what you two have been up to. Rand has given me updates here and there, but evidently, you made huge gains yesterday before the attack," said Bannon.

Rand and I took turns presenting our discoveries, ending with what we believed was the entrance to Cali Bantu. Rand concluded by saying we should travel to this location with haste.

"I agree. We need to form a team, and set a departure date," Gray responded.

"I want to be on that team," I said. "And you need me to go. I can recognize the clues to find the access, which will be riddled with protective devices. And once you're in, there will be more booby traps. This place was designed to prevent everyone, but those trained from entering. As far as I know, I'm the only one you have. My grandad said more kids were being trained, but evidently, they aren't here. I'd know. And if you knew who they were, they'd be in this room."

They all stared at me in disbelief, and Bannon was fiercely shaking his head.

"How do you think a conversation like that would go with your parents, Connor?" asked Haru with more emotion than usual. "Do you think they, or we, would endanger a child? This mission will be treacherous."

"He's right, Connor," Gray said. "We don't know half of the threats we will encounter."

"I realize the Corporates may be on our tail, and maybe we'll encounter enemies and dangers we aren't even aware of. But that doesn't negate the fact that you need me to be on this mission. I've already researched traveling during the fall in this very area," I answered. Rand used his hand to suppress a snicker, but he quickly regained his composure when three disapproving glares were sent in his direction.

"Of course, you have," Bannon sighed, leaning back in his chair.

"I would show you, but my tablet has been wiped clean, and realizing we were dumping classified material, I destroyed my notes and maps in the compost toilet. But I can replicate them from memory."

"Oh, good grief," said Gray. "Connor, we can't. We just can't." He threw his arms out and shook them in confirmation of his stance.

"Look," Rand reluctantly interjected, "I hate to say it, but he's right. I've been working with him. He knows dozens of codes, symbols, and steps for solving problems. Without him on site, there is little hope of completing this mission. It's not fair that he's just a kid, but he's the only one who can access Cali Bantu and retrieve whatever is in there."

Bannon got up and walked back to the water cooler to fill the pitcher. He flipped something in his mouth and filled his glass. He tipped it, drinking it all in one swallow like a saloon cowboy in a Western movie.

"Protecting you has been one of the most difficult jobs I've ever had," he said wearily. "Your curiosity is intense, but unfortunately," he sighed, "we need it. I know your grandfather taught you solutions to clues that only you understand, solutions we desperately need to achieve this goal. It would be hard enough to risk your safety for this town, this territory, and beyond if you were an adult. But that you're just twelve years old makes it an impossible task. That being said, I'm afraid you *are* the one who can help us. Though I hate everything about it, those who enjoy freedom have the responsibility to maintain it. As young as you are, you have been burdened with the task."

I was pretty sure that was a yes, and excitement surged through me.

"Bannon!" Gray barked. "You cannot be serious!"

"You think I like it, Gray? My own son was born less than twenty-four hours ago," he bellowed. I had never seen him so upset. Slamming down his empty glass, he leaned heavily on the table, and I worried he might collapse. "I can't even imagine the conversation I have to have with his parents. Nor do I have any idea what to do if they, very reasonably, refuse to allow it. This whole thing is untenable.

"I'm not sure if I'm thankful or angry that Deegan trained him. But shall we lose everything when we have a shot, or worse lead the enemy to it because we're unprepared? If they have half the information we do, you can bet with their camp of Highminds, they'll figure it out." Bannon folded with exhaustion into his chair. He had been up for a long time with the battle and the birth of his son. He seemed to shrink into the difficult place at the head of the table.

I imagined how I would feel about sending Mesh into danger or having to tell my mom she needed to go. It reminded me of a Shakespeare quote my grandad used to say. *Uneasy lies the head that wears a crown.* But as citizens, we depend on our leaders to make those hard choices.

"Well, we could try and come back for him if we need to," Gray argued.

Haru piped in, "I think Bannon's right. We get one shot at this. And for the sake of all, including Connor, it needs to be our best attempt. And Bannon, let *me* talk with Henry and Rhinda."

"I don't want you to worry about credits," I said, playing my last card. "I just want scooters for me and my three friends." I tried not to smile at my win, but I was going on an adventure.

"For Pete's sake! You're making deals with your safety! This isn't a game, Connor," Gray said, holding his head in his hands. "Let me make one thing clear, Bannon. I'm going on this mission! Gabe can take over for me."

"Okay, Gray, I know Jilly is pregnant, and leaving her is a huge sacrifice, but I agree," said Bannon. "Well, we have two so far. Gray, can you have a preliminary list of your team members and required supplies to me by Saturday morning?"

"I can get them to you tomorrow." Gray told him. I could tell he was angry, but it wasn't at me. It was for me.

I turned to Rand, who was sitting to my left, and whispered, "So do you think I'll get my scooters before we leave?"

"Dude," he laughed and whispered back," that was a brilliant move. What you're asking for doesn't compare to what you're giving in return, but let Haru talk to your parents first."

That evening, Bannon held a town meeting at Treagan Park to address the unrest about our new alliance with the Fringers. He started his speech by reassuring the residents that they destroyed many of the main roads, that the Corporates would need to access New Haven. It was unlikely the Corporates could transport a large army before the roads were repaired, and that couldn't be done until the snows receded. With the supplies, recycling programs, and their small manufacturing plant, as long as they could keep the tunnel secure, they could live unchanged for the next year and a half.

"After that," he stated, "the most important thing to consider is this. We have been discovered. Defending this town is going to be difficult."

"We, your elected officials, voted unanimously to support the Guard faction for three reasons. First, we cannot protect our town after the winter snows melt without an ally. We may still be attacked, but it will be harder for our enemies to overtake us with our united armies. Second, the Guard has more than twice the number of soldiers we have. Third, they manufacture weapons and ammo. They use an old technology, but it is effective, and it triples our stores and manufacturing efforts. They have connections for trading and gathering supplies, and they're willing to trade with us."

It was Gray's turn to talk. He relayed news from William and reiterated Bannon's message of the battles to come. "The Guards have underground connections within the territory cities. We have many drones between ours and the ones at the Hold. Together we have a strong first line of defense."

Many hands rose to be recognized and heard. I couldn't help but contrast this scene with the one we grew up with. All we were offered were edicts on how to comply. Not complying meant one's weekly allotments, which were barely enough, would be withheld, and the punishment extended to those who offered assistance. In other words, not complying meant starving. It was how the people outside still lived.

"How can we trust him? We don't know him?" shouted one man.

"How can we not? If he wanted our town, he could have taken it," Bannon answered.

"Why didn't you even consult us?" a woman asked.

"They had to leave by morning to beat the storm. We didn't know how bad it would get, or whether we would have an opportunity before winter closed us off. The storm is still ongoing, and it could take three or four more days to clear up and longer to plow our roads. It was a decision made in combat. The legislators have that authority when the danger is high, and there isn't time to go through legislation. The enemy never breached our town, so they still don't know what we have. But that day could come, so we must do everything in our power to prevent it." Gray saw many nods, and they seemed more contemplative than agitated.

Bannon spoke again. "Our creed has been like our mission statement. We protected the town and its location by sacrificing our freedom to leave and engage with the outside world.

"I built this town because I wanted to revive the dream of self-governance. I wanted to provide a safe place for new opportunities, career choices, and self-determination, but it falls short of the true goal of New Haven. Yet, this is just the beginning. It's time to expand this dream and remember our purpose and our goals.

"I have something to tell you. There are more towns like this out there. I know dozens of business owners who were working on places like this. I don't know where they are, or if they still exist. None of us ever divulged our locations, but I can only hope that someday we can work together to free everyone.

"We abandoned the rest of humanity to find our own. I pray we will be forgiven for that, but I still believe it was the right thing to do. I can only hope we had it long enough to treasure it and teach it, and love it enough to fight for it and keep it alive." Bannon paused and bowed his head. He looked consumed with troubles. "What we need to work on is a new mission statement together. Does anyone have any ideas of what we should include?"

The suggestions poured from the crowd, overlapping one another in exuberance.

"We need to make more things."

"We need to help the people on the outside."

"We should share our educational programs with the children of the Guard."

"I say we should stage another accident and stay in here and do a better job of protecting it this time."

"What kinds of supplies do we need? Could we find others to trade with?"

"How can we find those other towns?"

We were asked to send our mission suggestions to the City Hall site. This is what freedom looks like, and losing it wasn't an option.

CHAPTER 24

I wasn't at the meeting where Gray presented the supply list and who would be on the team. Rand and I were focused on the best route as well as alternate ones. Most of the team would be traveling in an all-terrain vehicle called the Brute, and the rest would be in smaller versions called Mini-Brutes. Gabe took me to see them.

These utility rigs had hydraulically changeable tires and snow tracks, heavy-duty winches, hydrogenic proton batteries, and electronic sensing radar. The dashboard was cluttered with buttons, gages, and other blinking instruments. Knowing how rough the roads were, and that winter was approaching, I was very excited to see the comfortable chairs and heated cabs. The Mini-Brutes only held two passengers, but they had significant storage room, while the big Brute was fitted with three rows of seating taking up much of its storage area. It made me wonder how many people would be going.

Axle was a day away from being released from the hospital. Since he had been on some of the roads we would be taking, Rand and I got permission to meet with him. He looked alert and happy, but he was still tethered to an I.V. bag.

"Little dude, nice score on the mission slot. I'm trying hard to get well enough to join you."

He'd be a good addition. I didn't see how they would let him, but then again, they were letting me. He was a strong, experienced soldier with extreme determination, and depending on when we'd be leaving, it may be possible. They hadn't even talked to my parents yet, but that would be soon.

Axle looked out of place in the clean white hospital bed while discussing the dangers of the area we would be traveling in. I could see he was frustrated with his confinement. As he talked, his excitement grew, and I imagined he was devising his own form of leverage to ensure his place on the team.

"Well," he stated, "the I-70 up to this point is in good enough shape for the Brutes, but there wasn't any snow when I traveled on it. Here, here, and here you might encounter avalanches. Also, there are a lot of Fringer tribes out there that will see rigs like these and think Corporate invasion. They aren't well-armed, but they aren't defenseless either.

"There are also bands of rogue Fringers that prey on travelers, using very effective traps. The team will be briefed, and the Defenders shouldn't have trouble dealing with them," Axle turned to me. "Connor, you must listen to everything they tell you for your protection as well as everyone else's."

As he continued to fill in the details, I could feel my enthusiasm and bravery fading, but I couldn't let anyone see that. I had to go. I was the only one who could get inside this... whatever. It might seem arrogant, but I wasn't feeling superior; I was feeling duty-bound.

That evening, Gray and Haru knocked on our door. Meshka had been conveniently invited to a sleepover with Ellie Vogel, Bannon's daughter. I had a feeling the proverbial fan would be causing quite a mess at any minute. I wasn't looking forward to this, and I worried that my parents had the power to terminate my involvement.

The explanation had my mother and father standing up from the table and yelling.

"He's only twelve years old! Even the Corporates didn't allow kids this age to become soldiers!"

"You should have been honest about what my son was involved with!" yelled my dad.

"Henry," Haru said, "I agree with you. This goes against every policy we have for children. For the record, he will not be a soldier on this mission; he will be under the protection of a team of soldiers. If there were anyone else who could complete this task, we'd be sending that person. But Connor is our only hope to find and accessing this cache. If we don't find this before the Corporates plan their next attack, we're all doomed."

"Look, I would feel the same way if someone wanted to take my kid on a mission like this," Gray said, "But..."

"You don't have children," my mother interrupted with a voice of terrified fury. "You can't know, and this isn't your everyday mission,"

"Well, though we haven't announced it, Jilly is expecting. Though I'm new to the responsibility of fatherhood, I feel it strongly enough to understand your anger and feeling of betrayal."

"You must have noticed," Haru said softly, "that Conner is not your everyday kid. He has extraordinary abilities, and due to his training and genetics, he inherited his grandfather's destiny," Haru calmly put his hand on my mother's back as she began to weep.

I sat next to my mom on the couch. "You and Dad risked your lives and ours to get us here. We weren't happy or living well, but you took us away from everything we knew, and it was terrifying. We went on a crazy journey to have something better. That's what I'm doing, Mom. I'm going on a journey to make it better for our family, and everyone."

"Oh Connor," she wept, "why didn't you tell me everything you were going through?"

"I couldn't, Mom. When I had GD, I didn't feel alone, but when he died, I just wanted to protect you. I thought when we got here it would change, but I discovered GD left me more secrets and I had to follow them. His destiny is mine now, and nothing can change that. But I'm glad you know now," I said with a shaky voice. Making her cry was breaking my heart, but not my resolve.

My dad was sitting with his head in his hands, torn by the impossible situation. He has always been more observant and intelligent than people gave him credit for. Looking back on my interactions with GD, it is clear my dad wasn't as oblivious as I had previously thought. He was smart enough to know what was at stake, but sacrificing his son to the cause was clearly beyond what he had imagined. And his regrets about that was killing him.

He stood up from the table where he had been listening intently. I could tell he was about to make his move. This was where he would refuse to let me participate. What that would mean, I don't know. And I wasn't sure what move the town leaders would take if he tossed that in the mix.

Gray saw my dad's determined approach, and he threw out one more persuasive pitch. "Rhinda and Henry, Connor is right. He has a destiny. He may be facing it earlier than anyone expected, but we're assembling a whole team to help him fulfill it. He will be accompanied by a medic and a squad of Defenders. One of them will be me, and you have my word, I will guard him with my life," Gray declared.

"Exactly what does this protection look like? How long do you expect this mission to last? Will there be any way to communicate with him during the mission?"

This was turning out to be much harder than I had anticipated. They never questioned letting Haru, Gray, and Rand step in and take over their parental roles before. It hurt me sometimes how quickly they passed me over to them, but this was different. It was a whole new level of abdicating.

Haru assured my parents and me that more meetings and explanations would be scheduled as soon as the details were solidified. Gray added that team members would be there to answer all the questions they could.

"Mom, Dad," I said softly. "I have to do this. It may turn out to be a straightforward short trip. I know it's a sacrifice a kid isn't usually asked to make, or a parent asked to agree to, but it's not like they're throwing me in a volcano or something." My dad huffed, and my mom smiled sadly through her sniffles. I suddenly found myself wondering if Pyramid Peak was geologically active. "I'll be okay," I said for myself as well as my parents. "I'll be back before you know it." She squeezed me in her arms, and my dad came and joined in the hug.

All my fears melted away in that moment. I felt ... important to them, and not just because I was their son. I always knew I was loved, but all my life I had to keep who I was from them. How could they love me if they didn't know me? They knew I was smart, but they didn't know what that entailed. I always imagined when the extent of my deception came out, they would be angry and hurt, and maybe, they would be afraid of the real me. But now they knew everything about me, and they loved me deeply and truly. I will cherish this moment forever.

I asked my friends to meet me at Wally's that Sunday. They were surprised when I gave them their scooters, each in a different color.

"How in the world did you swing this?" Hayden asked with a look of confusion and suspicion.

"I got an advance for a project I'm working on," I answered, trying not to intrigue them too much. It made me consider how hard it would be to say goodbye to them. I knew I'd be the only kid on this mission, and the loneliness of it began to take hold of me.

"That must be some project," Teke quipped, looking at his new shiny blue scooter.

"Yeah, some project indeed," Hayden said under worried breath.

"The tires still have the new knobs on them," Kato said, bending down to admire his forest green prize.

"I love this orange," said Hayden. "We've got to owe you something for these, Condor-Man."

I began thinking about the monumental cost of these runabouts. As if seeing my brain agitating through a difficult cycle, Hayden suggested we take a long ride. We rode all over town until we came to Brad Anderson Middle School Park. They parked their new rides in the bike rack, and I followed them with my black scooter streaked with silver lightning bolts. Gray special ordered the decals, making my ride one of a kind. It was more evidence of the unthinkable ask.

We pumped on the swings while making guesses about what jobs we might want and taking bets on who would get a girlfriend first. I had never told them about Sandra because it still made me feel foolish. I was calmly brushing away their inquiries, saying I hadn't decided what I wanted. Inside, I was thinking I might not even have a future. I was involved in a heavy purpose to ensure everyone else got one, and the price was settling in.

I looked at my friends. They were carefree and dreaming of futures. While I'm gone, they will play ball, go to school, ride around town, and sleep in soft beds. It wasn't just my safety and comfort that I would miss; I would miss everything. Teke and Kato went home while Hayden and I remained on the swings.

"Look," Hayden said with sincerity," we have always allowed each other the space to hold secrets, but Connor, something is very wrong here, and it's eating you alive. You've hung around the tall people way too much. You need to spill it before you lose yourself. I'm good for it. You know I am."

I left the swing to sit in a large cylinder leading inside the dome-shaped jungle gym. Hayden followed me. I poured out everything. I know I shouldn't have. I should have protected him, but I needed to fall apart. If I did it in front of the adults, they'd prevent me from going. If I didn't go, no one would be spared. I guess I wanted to see if, like my parents, he would still like me if he knew the real me.

He sat stunned for several moments, and I began regretting my selfish purge.

"Holy...," he said, shaking his head and blowing out a long breath. "I honestly wasn't expecting anything like that. You should have confided in me."

"I know," I sighed. "I just didn't want you to worry or be a target. Ever since I found GD's stash, I've wondered why he would enlist a child to save our territory."

"He was probably thinking he had no choice. You were born into his world, and you fit the mold perfectly. I'm sure he agonized over it, and he rationalized it by believing he would make it to New Haven."

Our moods were serious and tense, but it was at last honest.

"Will you be able to contact home at all?" Hayden asked.

"I don't know. I'm told things as I need to know about them. Like tomorrow, instead of going to school, I begin classes in self-defense and firearms, as well as being fitted for a Defender vest and helmet." I felt my chest tighten at the thought of having to fight someone or pull the trigger and kill them.

"I have thought of all the ways this expedition could go wrong, but I hadn't owned it, til now. I'm scared, more scared than when I was traveling from place to place to get here. Don't let anyone know I said that. I don't want them fawning over me, or pulling the plug on my going."

"Well, they're going to worry over you, but it sounds like they can't pull the plug," he said.

"Oh yeah, did I tell you Jilly is expecting?" I said, interjecting a piece of happy news into our tense exchange.

"Well, that means Gray isn't on the team," Hayden said, and I flinched. "Whoa, he's going and leaving her?"

I held out my hands. "When I researched on my own, everything was in my control. Now, everything is out of my control. I feel like I'm in a barrel rolling down a mountain, and no matter what I do, I just keep tumbling."

"Like a Greek hero with an unavoidable destiny," he said. "No matter what happens, that's what you'll be, a hero."

"Not if I fail," I held back a sob. "My only homage will be as a tragic martyr. And I'll be blamed for the evil things that happen to everyone here." I began to cry.

"You give us hope," Hayden said, putting his arm around me. "You are undertaking something no kid should have to. The talls will carry the blame for any failure, not you, and they should. But you won't fail, Connor. It's not something you do."

"It cracks me up that you call adults talls," I said, relieving the tension radiating from the playground tube.

CHAPTER 25

I was given a round of vaccine shots to protect me from the common viruses lurking outside the tunnel. At least, it was Dr. Mya's best guess of what was outside. Though we didn't plan on stopping at many settlements, we would be stopping at Breckenridge. It was the Fringer town between New Haven and the Hold.

The shots didn't hurt. They just stung a little, but I was given a couple of pills for the pain. I rolled my eyes at anyone who couldn't take a couple of stings, but later, my arms ached horribly. I couldn't fall asleep until I took the medicine I had been given. The next morning I woke up with chills and a headache, but they were almost gone by dinnertime.

The news reported that William of the Guard and a couple of his people were coming to visit the tunnel. They weren't going to be taken to Town Hall until they were given a tour of the town. One of the Fringer soldiers had been too injured to return to the Hold and had been admitted to our hospital.

I passed them while leaving the hospital after my physical. Gabe was taking them to see their soldier. One was medium height with dark hair, and he was taking in his surroundings with an intense interest. The other was about six feet, like my dad. He had a kind face, a friendly manner, and a smile to match. The third one was William.

He was seriously tall, and his well-built physique tugged at his clothing. He had rich dark skin and haunting eyes tinged with green and brown hues. When he walked into a room, he owned it. He oozed power and demanded respect without uttering a sound. I truly hoped he was on our side because he looked dangerous.

So many things were changing. We had been required to spend four weeks in the Hold to make sure we weren't carrying any illnesses. When we shut the gates to New Haven so many months ago, we believed no outsiders would be let in our town. Within the last six months, we had welcomed seven offsite Defenders, a Fringer refugee, and now four more Fringers had breached our sanctuary. I'm sure they were only here to get their soldier, but it felt like we were open for business, the infectious kind.

The next day I was brought to Town Hall again. I was a complete no-show at school these days, sore from my self-defense classes, and running out of lies about what I was up to. When I walked in, the familiar foursome of "talls" were waiting.

"How are you doing, Connor?" Haru asked with a probing look at my wince as I took my seat.

"I'm okay, just a little sore," I said, but he could tell my muscles weren't the only cause of my discomfort. He knew I was worried.

Gray flatly said, "I hear you're doing well in your self-defense classes. The soreness will wear off. But you'll feel more confident knowing you can defend yourself if you need to." He looked more than irritated. He looked ready to defend his corner. I hoped it wasn't anything I had done.

"It's perfectly normal to feel apprehensive before a mission," Haru stated. "We will have a meeting with you and your parents before you take off. But I will also meet with you alone as a follow-up." I took that to mean he would address those concerns I was trying not to worry my parents about.

"I should be the least apprehensive. I'm more protected than any of the others. But it would be nice to ask questions without worrying my parents or taking up meeting time." I thought for a moment and asked,

"Are all our notes gone? Should I rewrite them and redraw my pictures of the mountain?"

"No," Rand answered. "We have a backup drive buried offsite. Gray and I already went there and turned off the lock. It's all back on our main drives now, and individuals can upload their tablets. But the info you had on yours hasn't been released yet."

"How are your parents?" asked Bannon.

"They go back and forth between frustration and worry until they are left with sadness. But I think they have come to accept that I'm going. We need to know what to tell people, though. All our friends think I have an incurable condition."

"We'll be more forthcoming with them before you leave," said Haru. "We don't want people to know about this mission yet. Today, we're here to fill you in on who is going with you."

"Oh, good. I've been curious about that. Gabe showed me the Brute and the Mini-Brutes we will be taking," I answered. "They're awesome."

"We have tentatively set one four days from today for departure. We are waiting for the road teams to return. They are ensuring that the roads between here and Denver are impassable, and the route we plan to take is clear. That should give us protection from any large squadrons reaching us or the town before late spring," said Gray.

"Oh, that's smart," I replied. He just nodded with a serious face. Something was up.

"The team has some people you know," said Bannon, "and some we will introduce you to. Gray will lead the mission. Under him will be Jax, Leo, Axle, Lana, and Easton. Axle and Easton will be on the sweep, so they'll leave a day or two after the rest of the team."

"What's a sweep?" I asked.

"That's the last troop that follows well behind the main convoy," Gray stated in a straightforward soldier voice. What in the world was bothering him?

"Gabe said we'd be taking four mini Brutes plus the big one. That's enough room for sixteen people, but you only mentioned seven names. That's a lot of room for seven travelers. I was hoping Rand was going. I need him to help me," I said. Though I had hoped for a larger convoy because it seemed safer. Maybe it was decided we should be less noticeable. But only seven, really?

"Yes, there will be more people, a medic for one. The one we initially chose got a new position at the Hold. So, we had to replace her today. Jilly will be the team medic."

Oh, there it was. That was Gray's mood maker. "How can she go? Isn't she pregnant?" I asked with concern.

"She lost the baby five days ago," Gray answered somberly.

"Oh Gray, that's so sad." I had been clinging to that happy news, and it was heartbreaking to hear they lost a child. It added grief to Gray's worries. The quiet that followed was heavy with unyielding pain, and there were no helpful words to say.

The Gray I knew didn't easily share such hard emotions in a group setting, and he was bound to end the bleak mood and fight his way back to the agenda. I wasn't surprised when he changed the room's tone by giving a frustrated response to end the unbearable sympathy. "It wasn't going to be easy when I had one charge to watch over; now I have two."

We all have to watch over each other, I thought. But I kept my words to myself. We all allowed him the jab without rebuttal.

"As far as the list goes," Bannon continued, "seven more people are going. William of the Guard, five of his soldiers, and his tech man are also on the team. That's twelve highly trained soldiers, a medic, a tech, and you."

I froze. The Fringer army was joining us? "How well do we know them?" I asked meekly.

"Well," added Haru, "William of the Guard has been hiding clues for the rebellion too, and he has brought them to us. He has a couple that we know pertain to Cali Bantu. One of those is the Sanguine Blade. He has kept it safe since he was eleven. Does that remind you of anyone you know?"

I smiled. If it *truly* was the blade from the scroll and the poem, it was a significant contribution. *If* proven, I promised myself I would reevaluate my biases. I asked to see it, but it was locked away.

I was disappointed to hear Rand would not be joining us on the mission. He explained to me that he had been working with Relic, the Guard tech, and he was more than qualified to assist me. Rand had extensive knowledge about the technology of the Hold and the town and was the only one who could run both, so he needed to stay. Haru gave me an appointment for the next day to talk about the parameters of the mission and my part in it. Then the meeting adjourned.

It was two days before our departure day, and again I found myself walking alone to think. I tried to focus on all the new places and exciting mysteries I would be involved in. But other times, I ran through all the dangers we may encounter, and the aching ball of fear expanded in my chest, constricting my ability to breathe.

When I got home, my parents were watching a news feed. The town's mission statement had been finalized.

It is the mission of New Haven to create and maintain a free self-governing town that can: generate and allocate supplies within a healthy environment; provide education and employment opportunities for all citizens; provide a strong defensive military; and maintain and seek out mutually beneficial relationships with outside allies.

It was well said, but the next story had my acute attention.

A young woman named Lana was assigned to be in charge of the new historian division. It was her job to collect stories and data from New Haven residents with plans to get them from our new allies. The name for our emerging nation was the United Citizens of Free America, but we first had to free Colorado.

I knew her name because she was on our team. Our mission was going to make it into our recorded history book. I wondered about her writing style and how much of the mission she would be allowed to report. So much of what we were doing was too secretive to disclose.

At home, I sat on my balcony watching people walk and ride casually by. They had no idea what was being planned, or how crucial it was to our survival. We couldn't share it, and we absolutely could not fail at it. I bowed my head. *Jesus, I'm so afraid, but I know I'm not alone. Please be with us all and help us bring love and compassion back to your world. Amen.*

I thought about future generations learning of this quest. I decided I would also keep a journal, and I added the first line to my tablet.

We set out with a hardened resolve, bonded with hope and strengthened by faith. On our shoulders, we carry the fate of freedom and the survival of the people.

JOURNEY TO CALI BANTU

Book 3 of the Highmind Series

Chapter 1

Good evening, this is Marcus Miller for New Haven Evening News.

We have a breaking story. In response to the attack several weeks ago, eight of our residents will be embarking on a mission of exploration. Their goal is to increase our military abilities. Though many of the details are classified, we can tell you who is assigned to the mission.

Gray Takota will lead the Defender team composed of Jax Nakano, Dom Draker, Axle Takota, Easton Mundy, and Lana Sheldon. Lana is a trained Defender, but she is also a journalist and will be documenting the journey as our town's historian. Jillian Takota will be the medical technician. The rest of the team will come from our Fringer allies and include their leader, William of the Guard.

But the biggest surprise is a child will be accompanying the team. At this time, we were not given a name, but the minor is twelve years old with unique abilities the team needs to be successful. This must be a very talented and brave young person to venture out into enemy territory. We can only assume he is needed very badly to justify exposing him to danger.

The report included a short interview with Lana and went on to say thank you and goodbye to three of our citizens. Dr. AnnDrea Channing, who was leaving the Rapid Aid Center to take over the medical facility at the Hold. Anyia Peters, the Fringer refugee, was also transferring to the Hold to manage their livestock. And Tanya and Haru were also traveling to the Hold. Tanya had spent her incarceration studying to be a minister. She planned to complete her degree while establishing a circuit ministry for the Fringers.

I watched the news feed as if it wasn't happening to me. It was too surreal to accept, too fantastic to be my life. Meshka looked at me with hero-worship admiration. Not like a big brother hero, more like a stranger she didn't recognize. My dad patted my back like he would a buddy. But I wasn't his buddy. I was his twelve-year-old son, and tomorrow, I was heading out on a dangerous mission. No one spoke. The only sound was the occasional sniffles from my mom as she held me in a tight embrace.

It was too intense, so I excused myself and went to my room. The real me was about to be outed. Everyone would figure out that the child was a Highmind, and by tomorrow morning everyone would know it was me. All my life I've had to protect my Highmind status, and when we moved here I chose to keep it hidden. I wasn't sure what life would be like when everyone knew. Maybe they'd be happy to see me go.

My grandad taught me how to maintain a casual façade to avoid attention. It eliminated the awkward division of being a genius and allowed me to spend comfortable time with my family and friends. I enjoyed the interactions, but lately, I have been physically isolated. I didn't attend school, and I only ate dinner with my family. I ate an early breakfast before going to physical training and had lunch by myself before reporting to Rand's office. That's where I spent the rest of my day until dinner. Gray made sure I had a couple of hours on Saturday and Sunday to hang out with my friends. My complete absence from school was rumored to be due to a medical condition or a mental illness. In truth, both were kind of true.

At this moment, the rumors about me implied that I was ill, excentric, crazy, or all of the above, but this report would transform me into a child freak/soldier. The report described the mission as one of exploration, which it was, but it omitted the search for a coveted weapon that would draw danger to us like a beacon.

The residents were smart enough to know it involved more than an impromptu romp through the perilous wilds outside the sanctuary, but I went from a sick and crazy kid to a tragic child being sacrificed for the cause. I'm not sure which image I preferred, but I was about to find out. My tablet started humming with messages, and a crowd of those who guessed I was the child was already forming in front of our house.

I had prioritized the people close to me at the top of the growing message list. My friends had written multiple texts demanding I reply. I started with texts from people I didn't know, not wanting to hear the hurt and panic from those close to me. A growing number of people were angry New Haven's "baseball hero" was heading into danger. Like the planning of our first game, this was evolving into a nightmare, only this was so much worse.

I didn't want to go outside, and my parents agreed, saying my friends should come here. Within minutes, they arrived carrying overnight gear. Hayden's whole family came. I wasn't sure if my mom or they made that decision, but I was glad my parents and Mesh had the support of their friends. I was happy my best buddies were spending the night. I wanted to spend every minute I could with them. After greeting my parents and settling their gear in my room, they unleashed their questions freely in rapid fire.

"How long have you known about this?" asked Teke.

"What exactly is this about?" Kato said.

"Are you scared?" Hayden probed. I had told him everything, and I shouldn't have, but he was playing along.

"I've told you guys about my grandad, GD. He taught me things that will be needed on the mission," I said.

I told them that on one of the missions, a forgotten language had been found written in several places in an area that they wanted to investigate. It was a language my grandad taught me. It was the explanation I had been told to say. It wasn't untrue, but it left out everything I knew they wanted to know, which qualifies it as a lie.

"Why don't they just take pictures and bring them back to you to read? Why do they need to take a kid with them?" Kato retorted. I could feel his ire rising.

It was a good question, and I saw this could go very wrong in a hurry. I had to shut this conversation down.

"If the message is about the surrounding area, they won't know what I need pictures of," I answered confidently. I didn't want to be viewed as a victim. I was a valuable member of an important mission. "I want to go. They didn't want to take me, but I convinced them they had to."

"Are you crazy?" blurted Kato loudly. "What did your parents say?"

"Well, they were pretty pissed, but Gray convinced them I'd be well protected. And yes, I guess I am a little crazy, but I'm excited too," I was trying to temper the mood and answer calmly. But inside I was a wreck.

"You're being awfully quiet, Hayden," Teke uttered with a tinge of irritation. "Our best friend could be heading toward his death, and you act like," he stopped mid-sentence. "It's almost like... wait. Did you know?"

I interrupted before Hayden could speak, trying to save him from lying. "He only knew I was working on a classified project at Town Hall, and I got in trouble for saying that." Hayden nodded at my answer. Now, he was lying. Here I am again tangled in secrets and trying to manage the fallout. Will there ever be a time when I'm not?

I shook my down-turned head. "Look, I wish I could spill my guts here. You deserve to know, but I can't. I'm sworn to secrecy. And so are you because I confessed to working on a classified project. Please don't take it personally. And unless you want serious trouble, don't say anything but what you read in reports. You may think everyone here is loyal and honest, but..."

"But what?" Teke demanded.

"Well, look what happened to me in the Hold and to Zoey when we first got here. And then Dewy was attacked. People are people, and sometimes they lose it." I was proud of that answer. It was logical and indisputable.

"Okay, but what are you looking for out in this old language-infested area?" Kato questioned.

"Bros before foes," I said while holding up my hands and shaking my head. They stopped their inquiries per our prior agreement, but I could see they were conjuring up their own answers and worries. "I am leaving in the morning, and I was hoping we could just hang out. I see you guys are ready to spend the night. Let's just have fun." I was on the verge of tears, and Teke put his arm around me.

"You never answered Hayden's question," Kato said. "Are you scared?"

"Honestly, I'm mortified."

Hayden covered his face while leaning on his hands, and Teke and Kato hugged me. This was as intense as telling my parents and just as painful.

Morning came early, and after exchanging our last goodbyes, I watched them fade down the tunnel as they headed to school. I packed my new gear bag onto the bus taking me and my family to the security building. My mom wanted to be with me until the moment we left the tunnel. They were led to the conference room, where they would wait until our briefing was over.

The briefing room in the security building was too small for the team and everyone involved in the mission, so we were bussed to the Legislative Room at Town Hall. It was a beautiful space, and I remembered wishing I could be here during official business, and here I was. Not sure this was what I had in mind. This was much more than just official business; it was top-secret business.

The meeting was a review of all the previous gatherings. The secure camp areas were discussed, as well as everyone's set-up duties. We would follow a prepared route to the Hold and pick up the Guards. They had gathered some reconnaissance information about the roads we would be taking. The approach to every aspect of this mission had a military drumbeat, and the strict discipline of the team members was palpable. I wondered if I was to be held to the same standard as these trained soldiers.

Jilly and Gray sat on either side of me. In our last meeting, Gray had responded to my condolences about the loss of their unborn child with a frustrated quip trying to hang onto his control. I understood him and didn't push further. I hadn't seen Jilly since I learned about her miscarriage. I wanted to reassure her and let her know I cared deeply and grieved with her, but this was neither the time nor the place. I grabbed her hand and tilted my head toward her. She gave me a sad but kind smile, which I returned with a knowing nod and a squeeze of her hand. It was more meaningful than any words.

Six buses were lined up in the columned alcove to take us back to the security building. The streets were filled with a hundred or more residents, all cheering and waving signs of support. We picked up and loaded our gear onto a cargo trailer and continued to the West corridor, passing many more well-wishers on our way.

Inside a large storage room poised before a large metal door were the big Brute and mini-Brutes ready to go. Several rows of Defenders stood at attention saluting us as we made our way to the vehicles. It was alarmingly similar to the formation they presented at Hannah's funeral.

My mother hugged me in front of the open door of the armored transport. My dad and Mesh joined in.

Mesh handed me a thick envelope and said, "We've been writing you letters and drawing pictures ever since we learned you were going on a trip. You can have them with you to look at whenever you want. They will work even if your tablet dies." The last word had her swallowing hard and sniffling back a cry. I found myself doing the same.

"You take good care of him," my mom said to Gray and Jilly.

"With my life," said Gray.

It was a strange hugfest. My mom was hugging my dad, and my dad was hugging Mesh, and all of them were hugging me. I guess they needed each other's support for a moment like this.

"I love you all so much," I said, trying to disguise the quiver in my voice. "I promise I'll come back to you, and every day, I'll think of you and know you're thinking of me." My mom gave me a last squeeze, and I got into the vehicle still waving and extending the goodbye.

Suddenly, my dad jumped into the Brute and took a seat next to Gray. No one asked him to leave. Everyone just went about their tasks. I looked at Gray, but he had an unapproachable expression, and he was already shifting the rig in gear.

Dear Reader, thank you for your support. Since this is an excerpt from a work in progress, minor changes may be made before final publication.

A CHAT WITH THE AUTHOR

What inspires me to write? Everything inspires me. It's exhausting. As a child, my dad called me his "what-if girl" because I envisioned endless scenarios for everything in my life. I used to call it my crazy side, but I quickly discovered that my introspective creativity allowed me to develop valuable connections and intriguing possibilities.

Why do I write science fiction dystopian novels? I love the paradoxical nature and intense drama in dystopian fiction. When dysfunctional settings are married with science fiction, it presents a possible future. When the hard-won advancements of society are destroyed or confiscated for power, it creates an opportunity for noble causes to flourish. Paralyzed with fear, the masses wait for a hero, one who possesses the duality of a selfless and compassionate moral code with a determined warrior edge. It feels purposeful to share the foreshadowing scenarios of this genre which go beyond recreational reading.

How do I develop characters? I use the traits I see in real people be they admirable, tragic, or despicable. I love hero quest stories that test everyday people in extraordinary circumstances. They are compelled to defend the vulnerable, but in doing so, they must cross the ethical boundaries that make them worthy. The characters I create are like children to me. I watch them grow and evolve. I grieve every time I cause them pain and misery or make them stray to advance my plot line.

For more information about Roxanne Ward visit: https://roxannewardauthor.com/

Acknowledgements

I am thankful to be in a nation where I can express myself freely. It is not this way for everyone. I write dystopian fiction as a tribute and a warning, that liberty is a concept, not a permanent structure, and it is our duty to protect it and pass it on.

In loving memory, I thank my parents, Harold and Carolyn, and I thank my family for providing me with a loving environment. I was raised where education and duty were revered, and individuality was encouraged. Because of their influence, I strive to continually grow and learn.

I thank my husband and best friend, Bryan, for standing by me and encouraging me. I thank him for being a wonderful business manager even though I am not an easy client. His focused attention to detail balances my endless creative ideas which do not always take a straightforward course. Through all that, he is still my biggest fan.

I thank my son Russ for his loyal support and for letting me use his son on my cover.

I humbly thank the Prichard Tavern for allowing my books to be displayed and sold and Keeley for being an awesome salesperson. I thank my business associates who guide me through the hard-knock ropes of the Indie author world. I cannot express enough gratitude to everyone who has offered support, suggestions, reviews, and help.

Bless you all, Amen.